FORBIDDEN LOVE

By the time Lyndal Frazer learns the identity of the stranger who rescued her and her sheepdog, Rowdy, from drowning, it is too late. She has fallen half in love with a sworn enemy of her ailing father. Torn between growing attraction and duty, Lyndal chooses family loyalty. But Hugh Trevellyn has made up his mind, too; a bitter feud will not be allowed to come between them.

Books by Zelma Falkiner
in the Linford Romance Library:

A SECOND CHANCE
RESTLESS HEARTS

ZELMA FALKINER

FORBIDDEN LOVE

Complete and Unabridged

LINFORD
Leicester

First published in Great Britain in 2005

First Linford Edition
published 2006

British Library CIP Data

Falkiner, Zelma
    Forbidden love.—Large print ed.—
Linford romance library
    1. Love stories
    2. Large type books
    I. Title
    823.9'2 [F]

    ISBN 1–84617–183–0

Published by
F. A. Thorpe (Publishing)
Anstey, Leicestershire

Set by Words & Graphics Ltd.
Anstey, Leicestershire
Printed and bound in Great Britain by
T. J. International Ltd., Padstow, Cornwall

This book is printed on acid-free paper

1

I tugged at the long, woollen scarf around my neck with one hand and at the same time ran the index finger of the other down the pages of the telephone directory.

'Come away from that phone, Lyndal!'

'Surely they won't mind being disturbed at this late hour when they hear what I've seen, Dad. It's useless calling the police. Getting them here in time is impossible,' I explained, stating the obvious. 'Tredrea, Tregonning, ah, here it is . . . Trevellyn, Tirra Lirra Pastoral Company.'

I reached for the wall telephone without looking at my father and went on.

'They could catch the thieves at it, for a change, instead of finding their sheep gone when daylight comes.'

'Didn't you hear me?'

I could no longer ignore the anger in my father's voice. He was beside me. I dropped my hand and turned to look into his very red face.

'But, Dad, we could be next!' I protested.

'No daughter of mine will have anything to do with the Trevellyns. I'd rather lose sheep myself than have that happen!'

Surprised by the strength of his outburst, I curbed the instinct to roll my eyes heavenwards and instead tried to talk reason to my father, to calm him.

'But the sheep stealing in the district is seriously out of hand, you know that. This is the first time I've actually seen someone acting suspiciously. It was pure chance I came home that way, and there they were, parked in among the trees down by Long Hollow.'

'What were you doing on that side of the river? You know I've always insisted on keeping away from their property.'

'What is all the shouting about?'

The appearance in the doorway of a short, dressing-gowned figure only added to my exasperation. My mother was sure to side with Dad to placate him. I went forward to meet her.

'I'm sorry, Mum. Did we wake you?' I smoothed down her tousled hair.

'No, I wasn't asleep, just dozing. I can't sleep until I hear you come in.'

This was not the moment to let guilt overtake me. I had to focus on the urgent matter that had brought on the shouting match, the glimpse of a dark shape up against the fence that ran down to the river.

Although I'd driven the last miles home at a breakneck speed that would have given my mother more cause for alarm, time was getting away — and so probably were the thieves, with a truck-load of sheep, especially if my headlights had spooked them.

'I was coming home from the township and took the shorter way through the State Forest.'

'That wasn't very wise, Lyndal,

especially at night. You could've hit a kangaroo or broken down and needed help. Did you take your mobile with you?'

My mother glanced across the room to the dresser.

'No, I thought not. I do wish you'd remember to carry it.'

Good one, Clarice Frazer, I thought, eyeing my mother. Make me feel real guilty. How can I confess I'd purpose-fully left the mobile at home? If I hadn't, you'd have kept up a barrage of calls about my estimated time of arrival right through netball practice. You couldn't help yourself.

'I hate the thing. It disturbs the quiet of the bush,' I mumbled.

'And that motorbike of yours doesn't? But you were in the truck tonight, so that's no excuse.'

Having had the last word, she bustled around the kitchen, filling a glass with water and shaking a pill from a bottle.

'Here, Alec, you really shouldn't get

4

yourself all worked up like this,' she scolded her husband, waiting whilst he swallowed dutifully.

It was enough to remind me of my father's precarious health, and feel even more guilty.

'I'll go and put the truck away in the shed. I was in such a hurry I parked at the back door. If I leave it there it'll never start in the morning.'

My gaze followed my parents' slow progress as they left the room.

'I'm sorry, Dad, I got carried away.'

He grumbled his acceptance of my apology.

'You're remarkably impulsive for a grown woman.'

A grown woman, indeed! He obviously had been waiting up for me, as if I was still a teenager and I'd been twenty for almost six months now. It was understandably frustrating for a previously active man to accept the restrictions of a heart condition that made him almost an invalid, dependent on the women in his life.

With his illness, my father's personality changed from genial to bad-tempered, and he'd become quite paranoid, obsessed with such things as the long-standing feud with our distant neighbour. All attempts to talk about it only enraged him.

The thought of my brother coming home soon and taking over some of the responsibility cheered me. It would be good to visit with friends and not have the constant worry of my mother, fearful of an emergency, waiting for my return.

Without knowing why, I slipped the detested mobile into my pocket, wrapped the scarf around my neck again and left the warmth of the kitchen. Outside, the reality of what I'd seen weighed on my mind. The Trevellyns deserved the chance to intercept the thieves, feud or no feud. If I used the mobile, Dad needn't know.

It was a long time before the distant phone was lifted and a gruff voice answered.

'I'm sorry to disturb you at this hour, but there is someone down in Long Hollow,' I began.

'You rang to tell me that?'

'Of course. I thought it was very suspicious.'

'And what is suspicious about campers?'

Standing in the chilly darkness, I could feel the warmth of my embarrassment flooding my being. My father was right, I was impulsive! Without thinking of any other possibilities, I'd jumped to a hasty conclusion, and acted on it! But who would be camping out in winter? I couldn't imagine. What was there to say?

'Yes, campers,' the voice went on. 'There at our suggestion, on Sergeant Dunstan's recommendation. And who is this speaking?'

The mobile phone felt like a hot potato in my hand. Why had I been so foolish? By making a phone call to a virtual stranger in the middle of the night and going against my father's wishes, all because I'd seen campers, I'd brought this about. If I hung up now, without saying another word, the Trevellyns need never know who their caller was. I could remain anonymous, an embarrassment to myself only.

It wasn't a polite thing to do but I did it anyway. Impulsively, without a thought as to whether the call was traceable or not, I clicked off.

The idea of someone camping out by the river on a winter's night niggled me. Were they genuine campers, perhaps retirees travelling around Australia? But why park in such an out-of-the-way area of the large Trevellyn property, away from all amenities? Had they asked for a remote corner to savour the unspoiled bush?

If that was their intention they'd chosen well. Long Hollow was off an unfrequented road that led to nowhere in particular, more of an access road for the Bushfire Brigade in emergencies. But something about the remembered sighting didn't quite fit. What kind of vehicle was the huge dark shape I'd seen if it wasn't a transport truck? They were familiar to me. I'd grown up watching them loading livestock for transportation to distant markets.

Another thing had me thinking. A midnight call usually caught an older person unprepared, fuzzy-headed, but the person who answered had grasped the point of the call immediately. Who could it have been? The voice had been gruff, but young. My limited knowledge of the Trevellyns was of a couple the same age as my parents, but, because their homestead was many miles away on another road, closer to a big town, they were seen in our township only occasionally over the years.

It was the same with their children. They'd been sent away to school at an early age, as Grant and I had. Perhaps the voice belonged to a jackaroo who lived in the house. That would explain it.

In the morning, I went to breakfast, determined to check out the corner of our property where it met the Trevellyns', to satisfy myself that Frazer sheep had not been stolen.

Dad, returned to good humour by sleep and medication, made no objection when I announced my intention of spending the day checking outlying boundary fences. He walked with me to the sheds, grinning as it took several tries to kick-start the motorbike. I let the engine idle to warm up while I released Rowdy, my sheepdog. Glad to be off the chain, and eager for work, he took a flying leap and perched behind me on the bike. With a wave to my father, I headed out from the homestead — towards Long Hollow.

It was a fine, crisp morning after days of rain, and I relished the fresh smell of the bush. About a mile from my destination, I unlocked a gate and came out on to the public road I'd travelled last night. Before long, it curved close to the river, and the lay-by known as Long Hollow.

In the old days, when drovers walked

their flocks over great distances to the markets, the Government Reserve had been one of the many along the stock route. It was a pretty enough spot for a stop-over. There was a quiet, still loop on the river, cut off from the main river by years of floods. On the other side of the wide expanse of the fast-moving river, the dividing fence between Frazer and Trevellyn properties marched up the hillock that formed the hollow.

I began to feel silly. Whatever or whomsoever I'd seen last night, there was no-one here now. Dismounting, I propped the bike. Rowdy was already exercising his legs, following the scent of a rabbit or a fox, but, always alert for my command, not straying far. I strode across the clearing.

This was no ordinary camping site the morning after. It looked more as if a circus had stayed the night, with the grass trampled beneath heavy equipment or animals. No campers in a recreational vehicle could have wreaked such damage, not in a month of Sundays.

The corner where Tirra Lirra, the river and the Government Reserve converged formed a natural holding-yard. It obviously had been an easy matter to throw down a loading ramp from the transport truck and secure it with steel stakes. I could see the holes left after the temporary arrangement had been pulled up.

Calling Rowdy to heel, I ventured through the damaged fence on to Trevellyn property. If our neighbours thought they'd directed innocent campers to the Hollow, they were mistaken. There was no doubt sheep had been stolen. All the signs were there, including a dead animal close to the river.

I walked over to inspect and spotted another, halfway down the bank. Had it fallen in the loading rush or been injured and thrown away as useless by the thieves? My heart sank. No-one deserved this, not even the Trevellyns.

Closer to the edge, the imprints of hundreds of hooves in the soft ground told a story. How many had been forced over the bank and drowned? I stepped forward to get a better view downriver.

Suddenly, the earth trembled and heaved beneath my feet. The already weakened bank broke away. Frantically, I grabbed for non-existent anchors, anything to halt my downward slide. There was nothing. I tumbled with a scatter of stones, bushes and great chunks of dirt, into the fast-flowing river.

The water was icy. Gasping at the unexpectedness of it, my mouth filled. It became even colder as I sank into the dark depths, beyond reach of the wintry sun. Down there, the numbing cold quickly penetrated my body, effectively paralysing me. My lungs were going to burst if I didn't do something quickly.

With a desperate kick, I thrust myself upwards and broke the surface, coughing and spluttering as I dragged in great gulps of air. Somewhere in the distance, above the roaring of my heartbeat in my ears, I could hear furious barking as Rowdy followed my progress from the river bank. Then the sound died away.

In the powerful undertow, it became a struggle to keep my head above water. I guessed there must be a place somewhere along the banks of the river where I could perhaps grab an overhanging branch and scramble to safety.

If only I could see! Underwater, my hair had been swirling around my head like river weeds, but now it clung to my face, blinding me. I had to clear my vision but, because of my coat, it was taking a lot of effort. Each jerky movement of my leaden arm as I dragged it up out of the water was bringing me into contact with something bumping along beside me. Was it another dead animal?

At last I could see what it was — dear, loyal Rowdy and I were being swept downstream together, his furious dog-paddle also ineffective against the strength of the current in the rain-swollen river.

I had to save him before he tired and was carried away beyond help. My hand went out to grab his collar and bring him close to my chest. Once secure against me, the busy legs gave up the struggle.

Not far ahead, I could see the river swung in a wide arc that threw up a sandy beach. It looked promising. I figured if I worked with the current, maybe I could reach it.

It was now or never. I couldn't stay afloat much longer, not with water filling every air-pocket in my clothes and turning my boots into dead weights on the end of my legs. I rolled over on to my back to use approved life-saving techniques, sculling with my free arm, fighting with the last of my strength to overcome the current's pull. To my surprise, out of nowhere, I could hear a voice encouraging me and then hands at my coat collar, tugging.

Daring to put down my feet, I found

the river bottom and tried to stand up. Unbelievably-strong arms clasped the dog and me against a solid body. Cold and weak-kneed with exhaustion, stumbling and at times almost falling, I let myself be helped out of the water.

Dry land had never felt so good! I collapsed on my side, gasping desperately, like a landed fish, my eyes closed, feeling the water drain from me. I could hear Rowdy shuddering himself dry. I put out a searching hand to touch him but he was gone.

Opening one eye, I could see him skidding along the grass, first with one ear to the ground and then the other. It seemed a pity I couldn't do the same to clear the sloshing in my ears, but I doubted I could even lift a finger. Deft but gentle hands were taking off my boots, then turning me over to remove the jacket that had restricted my movements in the river. I opened another eye and gazed up into the face under the brim of his hat.

'I just got to you in time, didn't I?'

There was no waiting for an answer.

'I think we should get your jeans off, too. Can you manage that?'

This time he did look for an answer, one eyebrow cocked quizzically over kindly grey eyes. He held up a coat for my inspection before going on.

'You can put this on. I'll get a fire going to dry our things.'

Our things? I struggled to control my rag-doll limbs, to sit up and get a better look at him. The front and sleeves of the all-weather jacket worn by the man kneeling beside me were wet. Dragging a water-logged girl and her dog from the river bank had done that. He was soaked from the waist down. Had he risked his life?

'How far did you have to wade in?' I asked, a little unsteadily.

He shrugged off my concern.

'There's a shallow bank there. It was the best place to catch you and your trusty mate here.'

He stood up and I could see he was tall, and bare-footed. Had he taken off his boots before coming to my aid? The thought of warm, dry socks on my icy feet became desirable. As if he could read my mind, he produced a pair, and boots as well.

'Get those jeans off, and the coat on,' he ordered, turning away towards a truck standing nearby. 'Sorry I haven't a towel. I hadn't planned on going swimming today,' he called. 'But I do have the makings of a fire with me.'

He brought a box from the truck and busied himself building a pyramid of dry twigs. I must've had a surprised look on my face.

'I always carry dry firewood. You never know when you need to boil the billy for tea,' he explained. 'Oh, you're having trouble getting those wet jeans off. Here, let me give you a hand.'

'No, no,' I protested, shivering as movement came back into my body and reaction set in. 'I think the fire is more important.'

'Can do both,' he said, bending to grab the bottoms of my jeans and tug vigorously, so vigorously, in fact, that I ended up on my back with both legs free and in the air!

I clutched at the stiff, oiled-cloth coat to cover them but he had already returned to his fire-making. Soon, the pile of twigs caught, and, fed by branches of dry leaves pulled from a dead tree, flared into welcome warmth. I moved on shaky legs to stand beside it, holding my cold hands to the flames.

'Are you all right?' he asked. 'You could slap yourself to get the circulation going.' He demonstrated. 'Go on, try.'

And you could try shutting up, I thought testily. I may have nearly drowned but I'm not an imbecile altogether. Immediate guilt followed the thought. This is another of my shortcomings — I hate being told what to do! The poor guy was doing all he could to hasten my recovery. I was so lucky he'd been nearby. Tirra Lirra was such a big property, stretching for miles in all directions, that this corner probably wasn't visited often.

'I'm sorry,' I said.

He seemed genuinely surprised.

'What for?'

I could hardly say for being ungrateful, could I? He didn't know I had been, even if only for a minute.

'For putting you to all this trouble,' I said, and meant it.

He waved that aside.

'I would've been stopping soon to make a cuppa, anyway,' he replied, deliberately downplaying his action.

Surely he wasn't embarrassed by my thanks. He didn't look the shy type.

'I heard a dog barking and came to investigate.'

We both looked at Rowdy, already curled up dangerously close to the bonfire, steam rising as his coat dried. Steam was also rising from the boiling billycan. My rescuer threw in a handful of tea and removed the brew from the flames with a stick under the handle. He produced a couple of clean metal cups from his box of rations.

'Which brings me to the question,

what happened to you? How did you both come to be in the river? Fall out of a boat?'

The first gulp of hot tea wasn't the only reason for the heat that welled up and coloured my face. The near-drowning had made me forget I shouldn't be there at all. I was deep in forbidden territory.

I wanted to flee, but how could I? My motorbike was miles away and, under this guy's stiff coat, I wore nothing but warm socks and overlarge boots. Desperately, I eyed my still-wet clothes draped over a fallen branch he'd pulled in front of the roaring fire.

Naturally, he wanted an answer. What could I tell him? That I was investigating? Hardly. He might connect that to my telephone call at midnight last night. I hadn't heard enough to remember if his was the voice that had answered, the conversation had been so brief. But I had to stop him asking awkward questions.

I took my time sinking down on to

the tarpaulin he brought from the back of the truck. A lunch-box followed. He threw another branch on the fire that sent it flaring skywards, and joined me.

'Do you always travel with a change of clothes, and meals, in your truck?' I began conversationally, noticing he was wearing dry trousers.

When had he changed?

'Of course! Anything could happen when I'm this far from the homestead.'

The homestead! Even though the one on Tirra Lirra was miles away, I felt nervous. What if one of the Trevellyns came along?

'Are you the jackaroo?' I asked to cover my awkwardness.

He looked at me oddly.

'Jackaroo? Er, yes. My name is Hugh.'

He put out a hand to shake mine. There was silence. I wasn't going to fill it by offering my name.

'Do you like working away out here?' I asked, leaning over to take a sandwich from the lunch-box.

'You must.'

There was a determined look in his eyes as he turned the question back on me.

'Me? Oh, no, I don't work out here,' I lied. 'Rowdy and I love to come into the bush and explore. He thinks he's a top rabbiter, but is really pretty hopeless.'

I laughed, a little falsely to my ears, and looked away, anywhere except into the searching grey eyes.

'So how are you travelling?'

I waved vaguely in the direction of the road and stood up.

'I must be going. I promised to be back to town in time for afternoon tea,' I said, feeling my clothes on the improvised clothes dryer.

They were warm, and still wet, but no longer dripping. It wouldn't be comfortable getting back into them but anything would be more bearable than this cross-examination that could only result in either lies or revelations.

'Wait a while. Your clothes aren't near dry yet. Look, my mobile is in the truck. Would you like to use it and let them know you'll be late?'

My mobile phone! It was gone, lying at the bottom of the river. Something good had come out of the morning after all!

I shook my head, gathering up my clothes.

Suddenly, I became self-conscious, aware of Hugh as a man, and of my bare body beneath his commodious coat. I decided to use it like a beach changing-tent but that proved awkward as I struggled with jeans that seemed to have shrunk.

'No need to make it hard for yourself,' he said, turning his back on me to rearrange things in the truck. 'I won't look.'

'I'm trying to stay warm,' I bluffed.

'Of course. I'll drive you back to the road when you're ready.'

I struggled on until I dressed and it was possible to undo his coat, fold it and make a pile, together with his dry socks and boots. There was another struggle to get my bare feet into my still-wet, uncomfortable boots.

At last, I was able to whistle up Rowdy and go to stand beside Hugh.

'Ready,' I said, looking straight at him, daring him to ask any more questions.

2

A blue-striped white police car was parked at the back garden gate. I rode on past it to the sheds, my mind working furiously. Had my father reported last night's sighting? No, he wouldn't have done that. His enmity towards the Trevellyns was too ingrained.

It couldn't have been Hugh who had notified the police. He had no idea of my identity or that I knew what awaited him at Long Hollow. As well, unless the policeman was already on the road, he couldn't have reached Balool before me.

So what was Jason Dunstan doing here? That was a puzzle, but there was an even more pressing question that needed an answer. How was I to get to the bathroom without being seen and quizzed? It would be easy enough if

Jason was in the living-room with my parents, but there was no way of being sure of that. The sound of the motorbike would already have alerted my mother.

I tied Rowdy at his kennel with the other dogs and worked my way around through the garden to the side veranda. If my mother followed her usual custom that morning, the French windows to my parents' bedroom would be wide open for airing. They were.

A loose floorboard squeaked as I crept through into the hallway. I paused, one foot caught in mid-air, hoping my mother's keen ears hadn't picked it up. No such luck!

'Is that you, Lyndal?' her voice reached my ears.

'Be there in a minute, Mum,' I called back, making for my own bedroom, and slamming the door closed behind me.

The first sight of myself in the mirror was a shock. It would take more than a minute to repair the result of the morning's adventure. My dripping, shoulder-length hair, squeezed and hastily hooked behind my ears when Hugh helped me out of the water, had dried into a mass of rats' tails and river debris.

Hugh! For a moment the realisation that he'd seen me looking like this dismayed me. It was just as quickly followed by relief that the jackaroo from Tirra Lirra and I might never meet again, not if I obeyed my father and kept off that road. Somehow that didn't please me either.

Aware of the need to present myself as coming in from an ordinary morning's work, and do it quickly, I abandoned the thought of a shower and shampoo. A basic wash and change of clothes would have to do. Applying the brush vigorously until most of the hairs on my head had been separated and fluffed up, I tied back the long, thick hair with a wide bow. One last look in the mirror convinced me I could carry off the deceit, for my father's sake.

'You took for ever, dear,' my mother

commented, coming out of the kitchen with a fresh pot of tea and an extra cup.

'It was pretty muddy down by . . . er . . . getting through some spots, especially in the gateways, and I was splattered all over,' I answered, following her into the living-room. 'Hello, Jason.'

The tall, athletic-looking policeman unwound himself from an armchair and put out a hand.

'Well, you'd never know, to look at you,' he said gallantly, picking up on my remark.

He remained standing as I went to my father and dropped a kiss on his head.

'Nothing unusual to report, Dad,' I said.

My father smiled and accepted another cup of tea from his attentive wife. I decided lying wasn't as hard as I expected, not when it was for a good cause, of course. I wondered how I'd go under intense scrutiny or questioning. I looked at the policeman. Would those admiring brown eyes harden if I committed a felony?

That made me laugh to myself. I'd been watching too much television. As if I'd break the law!

'Jason was just passing and decided to pop in and say hello,' my mother informed me, favouring the visitor with an approving glance as we settled.

I had to admit it all seemed spontaneous, especially when the talk turned to local matters and eventually, to football. At last, the visit was over, without mention of sheep-stealing. I found that surprising. It was discussed often enough between landowners when they met. Perhaps the subject had been covered before I arrived home.

'Why don't you see Jason out, Lyndal, while I clear up?' my mother suggested, as he made his goodbyes.

'I wanted to ask you something without your parents being there,' the policeman began as soon as we stepped out on to the veranda.

So there was a reason for the visit! I

held my breath. What was he going to ask? Was I being dragged into police enquiries? Had I been seen at Long Hollow after all? Or had our truck been recognised on the road going into the forest last night?

What would be the effect on my father's health when he found I'd ignored his wishes, not once but twice? I tried to cover my apprehension with a smarty-pants remark.

'Are they too young to hear what it is?'

Jason smiled, showing a line of even white teeth. He certainly was attractive, for an older man, that is. My friends in the township and I had been talking about that since he arrived months ago.

'No. Actually, they don't qualify for what I have in mind.'

He paused to allow me to laugh at his joke, which I didn't get. Whatever was this about?

'Would you come ... ' he began, then paused.

Nervousness caused me to try a bit more humour.

'Down to the station to help us with our enquiries?'

It was the policeman's turn to look puzzled. We weren't on the same wavelength, that was clear.

'No, I wanted to ask you about the Bachelors' and Spinsters' Muster,' he said.

I was so relieved I became a little over-enthusiastic with my reply.

'I hear there's a band being imported from the city this year. That should liven things up.'

Too late, I could see unrealistic hope in his eyes. Right now, with my father so ill, the last thing I needed was someone becoming interested in me.

'Then you'll come with me?'

I couldn't very well back out at this stage, with him looking positively delighted, could I? I consoled myself with the thought of arriving at the muster with such a good-looking partner. It would cause a stir among the girls of the netball team I played in.

'Why, yes, thank you, Jason. That is, if my father is well enough and our visitor arrives.'

Jason looked puzzled again.

'My brother will have returned from the United States by then and brought her from Sydney with him,' I explained.

'And she wouldn't want to go to the muster?'

I had a sudden picture of my father's mother, the matriarch of the family, and a stern churchgoer with very decided views.

'It's Grandmother Frazer. She doesn't qualify either, nor does she agree with dancing or the drink.'

'Well, I do. This is my first muster and I'm looking forward to it!'

'You might be in for a surprise, city boy,' I promised. 'They not only work hard but they play hard out here in the bush.'

★　★　★

Jason Dunstan and the striped police car were often at Balool after that first visit. I became accustomed to returning to the homestead and finding him talking with my father. He seemed genuinely interested in how the property was run and Dad was certainly glad to pass the hours explaining farming practices to the city man.

When Jason appeared at netball practice, it was accepted among my friends that he was there to watch me. The girls in the team teased me unmercifully. Only Bobbie held back, turning away from the group with a strange look whenever the police car nosed into the parking area near the courts.

'What is it with Bobbie?' I asked Louise, my best friend. 'She seems to have a thing against Jason.'

'Well, you could say that,' Louise answered. 'For a while there she thought he was interested in her. It didn't come to anything, but he was very good to her family when they had sheep stolen.'

The whistle blew for practice to begin and when I looked again the police car was gone and with it, all thought of sheep stealing.

Nothing more had been said between Jason and me about the upcoming Bachelors' and Spinsters' Muster. The talk and planning at Balool was centred on the arrival home of my brother, Grant, and with him, Grandmother Frazer. I was looking forward to driving to the regional airport to collect them.

'Jason has offered to go over to Wagga to pick up Grant and Mother,' my father announced a day or two before the due date.

'What a pity he can't use the police car,' my mother commented with a rare flash of devilment. 'That would give your mother a heart attack.'

She turned away to hide the smile on her face. My father was not amused. I wasn't pleased either. The idea of Jason being there for such a family occasion didn't sit well with me at all. And if I knew my brother, he would be keen to get behind the wheel for the return journey. Like most Australian males, the Frazer men did not like being passengers.

'It's very good of him,' my father remarked, ignoring his wife's wisecrack. 'Take a bit of the load off you, Lyndal.'

Right now, the only load I wanted taken off me was Jason Dunstan. The cheap thrill I would get from going to the muster with him had already lost its appeal. Too much of a good thing, I concluded, thinking of the long drive to the airport alone with him.

As it happened, Jason proved to be interesting company. The time passed quickly and we arrived at the airport just in time to see the plane land.

Although my brother had been in the States a year, he hadn't lost the lean, rangy look of the Australian bushman. He ambled across the Tarmac, unself-consciously carrying our grandmother's hand luggage to allow her freedom with her walking-stick.

I was so excited to see him I quite forgot the regulations and ran beyond the terminal barrier to throw my arms around him.

'Hey, hold on, let me get into the building first!' Grant protested, struggling with hold-alls and duty-free bags. 'And say hello to Grandmother Frazer.'

I'd hardly noticed my grandmother, and she knew it, standing beside my brother with a long-suffering look on her face. It wasn't a good start.

'Grandmother Frazer,' I exclaimed, trying to make amends, leaning forward to kiss her proffered cheek.

My father's mother had lost nothing of her upstanding demeanour in the years since I'd last seen her. She wore her uniform of black, well-tailored suit with a froth of white lace at the neck and the inevitable black, head-hugging cloche hat. It wouldn't come off until we reached Balool.

I remembered my manners just in time and introduced our driver. After queries were made as to her comfort, we set off on the long drive home, with Grant in the front passenger seat and me in the back with my grandmother.

The time did not pass as easily on the return journey. Grandmother Frazer had many questions and often my answers did not meet with her approval. It was quite a minefield.

She had never forgiven our parents for the rôle reversal they'd allowed their children. According to her, Grant should be taking over from Dad, not me. I think she envisaged me as a receptionist, tottering around an air-conditioned office in impossibly high heels and a cloud of expensive perfume, or better still married, living in the upmarket suburbs of some city.

I could hear Jason was asking Grant questions, too, but my brother's answers seemed to amuse him. There was a lot of laughter coming from the front of the car.

It was late that night before I had a chance to talk with my brother. He expressed alarm at Dad's condition, and Mum's nervous state.

'You look a bit strained yourself, kiddo,' he remarked, following me into the kitchen.

'I must admit it has been a tough time.'

I prepared cups and saucers for a last cup of tea, and stood leaning against the sink, waiting for the kettle to boil.

'Well, it's over now. I'm here to share the load,' he said, enveloping me in a brotherly hug. 'Grandmother Frazer will be a help, too.'

I stepped back and looked at him incredulously.

'Grandmother Frazer, a help? Come off it, Grant. She's become part of the problem. Mum has been dreading her arrival. You can't imagine the preparations!'

Grant laughed that off.

'They'll get on like a house on fire, you wait. Having another woman in the house . . . '

'Thank you very much, brother. I am a woman.'

'OK, I'm sorry. You are a woman. Speaking of which, is this a man/woman thing between you and Jason?'

The kettle whistled and I was momentarily saved from answering, but Grant wasn't one to allow unanswered questions.

As soon as we'd pulled out chairs and sat down at the kitchen table, he asked again.

'It's funny, but it's not,' I confided, glad of a chance to talk about something that had bothered me. 'I've promised to go to the muster with him, and he's here a lot of the time, but it's not a man/woman thing. He seems to prefer Dad.'

'Do you mind?' my brother asked through twitching lips.

'No, not really.' I thought about that for a minute. 'Perhaps my ego is suffering a little,' I admitted.

'He's a fair bit older than you. Do you think he's being considerate?'

That suggestion made me laugh.

'Get real, brother!'

We sat for a moment in companionable silence before Grant spoke.

'I met a girl.'

Avid for details, I bombarded him with questions.

'Wait up, and I'll tell you. She's American, of course. I met her at one of the Harvard big weekends. Her brother invited her and we just hit it off straight away.'

A sudden fear struck me.

'Is it serious? You're not planning on going back to America, are you?'

'No, no.'

'No, no, what?'

'Well, no. It's not a man/woman thing either, and no, I'm not going back, especially not now. You and Mum have been managing on your own long enough.'

I wondered if I imagined the wistful look on his face. He got up and took his empty cup to the sink and turned.

'Look, it's late. I have plans but how about we talk in the morning? It's been a heck of a long day.'

★ ★ ★

On the night of the muster, Jason didn't get back from an outlying homestead until late. I had to sit and wait in the police station in my new evening dress while he completed his paperwork. He was all apologies.

Although I was dying to join the excitement of the night ahead, I reassured him.

'It couldn't be helped. Everyone knows a policeman's job means unforeseen emergencies.'

He made some flattering comments about my dress, which became a little tiresome with repetition. When I brushed them aside impatiently, wishing he would get on with his reports so that he could go to the muster, he explained.

'I'm like your grandmother, old-fashioned about girls wearing dresses a bit more often, instead of jeans.'

I flashed him a half-scornful look which put him on the defensive.

'Not on a motorbike or in the sheepyards, of course,' he added, stammering in his efforts to make himself clear.

'Of course not,' I agreed, laughing at his discomfort.

We could hear the band from the city belting it out long before we reached the old School of Arts hall. The paddocks on both sides were stacked with vehicles of varying makes and ages, many dirty from the long distances they'd travelled. Driving a police car meant Jason was able to park right in front of the door, by now choked with bodies coming out for a cigarette.

The stark walls of the old hall had been decorated with branches of eucalyptus, and glittering, iridescent balls hung from the rafters, adding a touch of glamour.

The floor was packed with energetic dancers, and it was almost impossible to locate the netballers' table.

'I told you the band from the city

would liven things up,' I shouted.

Jason bent his head close to my ear to reply.

'It might have been an idea to take lip-reading lessons before coming.'

The band stopped and the dancers returned to their tables. I waited until the floor was clear before leading Jason across it, in full view of anyone who was interested. As I hoped, the netballers were!

I had this sudden image of Grandmother Frazer's disapproving look. No doubt she would have reprimanded me for such a shallow, vain gesture. That wouldn't surprise me. Nothing I did was right. She'd even criticised the formal dress I wore as being less than demure, although that wasn't the word she'd used. Cheap it certainly was not!

Grant had been wrong. Her arrival hadn't helped one little bit. I shook off thoughts of home and the atmosphere there. This was the big night of the year and I was determined to have a good time.

The band left the stage for a supper break and some local musicians struck up the music for an old-time favourite, a progressive barn dance. I always enjoyed this part of the night. It was a good chance for a brief exchange of news with everyone, some of whom I hadn't seen since last year — and to meet strangers.

I wasn't the only one with this idea. The level of excitement in the hall was rising. I swung easily out of Jason's arms to my next partner and began the slow progress around the floor. Although I expected to meet some strangers, I wasn't thinking of the jackaroo from Tirra Lirra. Still chatting to my last partner as we changed, I twirled into Hugh's arms, unprepared for the shock of coming face to face with my rescuer. Surprised grey eyes met mine.

'Hello! You do scrub up well,' he drawled, taking my hand, and encircling my waist with an arm. 'I almost didn't recognise you.'

I performed the dance steps without stumbling, but remembrance of the day we first met, when I was looking my absolute worst, retching up river water, brought colour racing up from the low-cut neckline of my dress.

The brief moments in his arms before I was swept on to the next partner were over, without me managing to say a word! But what could I have said? Had he connected me with the late-night telephone call yet? But more importantly, had he found out who I was? He wouldn't know of the life-long feud between the Trevellyns and the Frazers anyhow, but he might've realised I'd lied to him about living in the township. Why should that matter, I asked myself.

'Hey, Lyndal, you've gone all quiet. What's up? Not having a good time?' my next partner asked, one of the guys from our table.

There was only time to apologise to him before we changed again, and I was in another stranger's arms.

With a fleeting smile for my new partner, I looked back over his shoulder to the line of dancers.

If I'd changed from a drowned rat to Cinderella at the ball for Hugh, he'd changed, too, not so spectacularly, I had to admit, but this suave figure in a dinner suit was a different person to my rescuer — not that I'd been in any mood to notice much about him at the time, being cold and uncomfortable, in the wrong place, and fearful of having my true identity discovered.

I twisted my neck to keep him in view as he smiled down at the parade of partners that swung in and out of his arms. His hair wasn't quite black, but a sun-streaked dark brown, slicked back from a face that was only lightly tanned, not weather-beaten. Obviously he hadn't been in the job very long, yet he seemed to know a lot of the dancers.

As he smiled and swung them in the dance, his eyes sought mine with every turn. I couldn't look away.

The distance between us widened

until it was no longer possible to meet his glance without it becoming obvious, especially to someone who knew me, like my brother.

'Something interesting you, Sis,' Grant teased, as I danced into his arms, 'or someone?'

I wished I didn't blush so easily. It was a dead giveaway, no matter how much I protested. I decided to ignore his remarks.

'Isn't it warm in here? Are you enjoying yourself?' I asked.

There was no doubt of his sincerity.

'It's great to be back,' he called as I moved on.

When the barn dance was over, Jason and I went to supper in the huge marquee set up especially for the occasion.

We returned from there to find a minor disturbance had developed at the next table and was spreading.

'This could get out of hand. I'll have to do something about it,' Jason warned. 'Will you be all right?'

'I told you they played hard in the bush,' I called after him as he moved away into the milling crowd, but he didn't hear.

From past experience I knew he wouldn't be making any arrests. There was nothing angry or malicious about this high-spirited free-for-all, just boisterous guys indulging in horse-play. Chairs were being knocked over and tables shoved around to make more room. It didn't bother me. I'd seen it all before. I stood back, out of the way.

A sudden surge of the crowd in my direction forced a table against me, pinning me to the wall. Its sharp edges cut painfully into my thighs. I pushed back, straining to ease myself out, but the pressure of the pack of jostling bodies made it immovable.

Just as suddenly, the table shifted again and I was freed. Hands pulled at my arm. I raised it defensively to shake them off. There was no way I wanted to join in the mêlée.

'Come on! Let's get out of here!'

someone ordered.

There was something familiar about the voice and, as an arm went around my shoulder, a familiar feel to the body I was pulled against. We stumbled our way to the nearest exit, Hugh and I, in a repeat of the scene by the river. Although the present situation had not been life-threatening, only uncomfortable, I felt I had to thank him.

'You seem to be always rescuing me,' I remarked as we came out into the starry night.

'It probably comes naturally, I suppose, to do with King Arthur and the Knights of the Round Table and all that.'

I glanced at him in the half-light from the hall, trying to remember the legends of Camelot and failing miserably.

'What has that to do with anything?' I asked, wondering if I had missed something.

There was no answer. Instead, he stopped and the arm around my shoulder tightened, turning me to face him. Before I realised his intention, his head bent to find my mouth.

'My reward,' he murmured. 'The fair damsel always allows the knight in shining armour a kiss.'

It was not one of your snatched, rough kisses from a stranger in a carpark, but a surprisingly gentle kiss that, just as surprisingly, left me wanting more. A crowd of noisy revellers burst out of the hall and came toward us, putting an end to such hopes.

I tried to appear unconcerned until they had passed, and we were alone again.

'What do you mean about Knights of the Round Table?' I asked through trembling lips, resisting the temptation to move back into his arms.

'Well, Sir Lancelot singing Tirra Lirra by the river. Don't you know the poem?'

Bemused, I shook my head. A jacka-roo in the Australian bush referring to poetry was something new.

'You do take your job seriously,' I remarked.

'And why not? After all, I am a Trevellyn of Tirra Lirra.'

3

It was as if there'd been a power failure and all my systems had blacked out. I stood stock-still, oblivious, unable to think or act, shocked out of my mind.

'Hey! What is it? Surely you don't object to me kissing you?'

His teasing voice re-activated my thinking processes. There was an immediate, unwanted remembrance of the announcement of his identity. Hugh Trevellyn of Tirra Lirra! I had no trouble understanding what that meant. It meant there could be no more kisses.

I took a step back, out of the reach of his arms. He went on, but more seriously.

'I've been wanting to do that ever since I dragged you out of the river. No, no,' he corrected himself, 'not exactly then, perhaps a little later, when you'd stopped — '

'I wouldn't go on, if I were you,' I warned, finding my voice.

'Why not? It was when you put out your hand to your dog although you scarcely had the strength to move. I thought, this is one special girl. And when I turned you over — '

'Stop!'

The shout was wrenched from me, but the music in the hall had begun again, almost drowning my cry. Hugh bent to look closely at me, and led me away gently to a quieter corner among the parked cars. He put his hands on my shoulders, forcing me to look at him.

'Tell me, what is wrong?'

'Do you know who I am?'

With a laugh, he tried to draw me back into his arms.

'No, as a matter of fact, I don't, but I've been banking on finding that out tonight. I guessed you'd be at the muster. How right I was!'

I resisted the pull of his hands.

'I am Lyndal Frazer.'

There was a flash of white teeth in the darkness.

'Well, hello, Lyndal.'

'Lyndal Frazer,' I repeated, parrot-like.

'Well, hello, Lyndal Frazer, if you insist.'

Why was he taking so long to catch on? Did I have to spell it out?

'Lyndal Frazer of Balool.'

It seemed I was through to him at last.

'Balool? Well, what do you know, my next-door neighbour! And here was I, hanging around the township whenever I could, hoping to catch sight of my mystery girl.'

He was chuckling, which really made me mad. It was no laughing matter, at least not for me. I'd been attracted to one of our family's enemies and I didn't like the idea of having to give up before anything really got started.

'I think we'd better go back into the hall. It sounds as if everything's normal again, and our partners will be wondering where we are,' I announced through unsmiling lips.

He dismissed that with a half-wave.

'I haven't a partner. I've been away so long I didn't know which of the local girls were still unattached.'

In spite of myself, I was intrigued.

'You've been away?' I asked.

'Yes. I've been in America, at Harvard University, getting myself a business degree.'

My sharp intake of breath broke into his consciousness.

'Frazer? Grant's sister? Of course. How stupid of me!'

I couldn't believe the co-incidence of two Australians, and neighbours at that, being at the same American university. The name of Hugh Trevellyn had certainly never come up in Grant's e-mails.

'You knew each other at Harvard?'

'Yes. Someone in the faculty mentioned there was another Australian on the course and I went to look him up. Naturally we hadn't known each other before because of going to different schools in Sydney — '

I cut him off.

'Yes,' I said, making it clear I didn't need to hear any more. 'Obviously, Grant has kept the friendship from us, and I suppose you thought it best not to tell your parents.'

'What are you talking about? Of course I told my parents. Why shouldn't I?'

Perhaps it suited him to pretend he knew nothing of the feud between our families. Whatever, anything between us was over before it started. I stifled a sigh and put on my best manners.

'I must go. Jason will be wondering what's happened to me. Thank you again for saving me from both the river and the free-for-all.'

'What are you doing here with that policeman?'

There was a rough edge to his voice that made me take offence.

'Excuse me?'

Hugh didn't seem intimidated by my haughty tone.

'You should've come with me. I'm younger and better looking.'

I stiffened at the truth of it, and turned to go, full of regret that he was a Trevellyn.

'Joke! Joke!'

With a laugh, he linked his arm in mine.

'Why are you always so touchy?' he asked as we threaded our way through the vehicles.

Touchy? If only he knew! It wasn't possible to explain that ever since we met I'd had to control my normal reactions. I feared discovery by the Trevellyns the day I'd fallen in the river, and now I feared a discovery of another kind. I couldn't let him see I found him attractive. My Frazer pride demanded that!

Jason was at the door, looking out into the night.

'Oh, there you are, Lyndal. There's a bit of a problem with Grant.'

There certainly was as far as I was concerned. He'd have to explain to me why he'd befriended Hugh Trevellyn at Harvard. No wonder he had kept it a secret!

'What kind of a problem, Sergeant?' Hugh asked.

Jason ignored him and addressed me.

'He's had a little too much drink to drive his car. I've taken his keys,' he said, handing them over. 'I think you should get him home. I need to stay here in case there are further developments.'

I suppose I half expected Jason's job might intrude on the evening, and somehow it didn't matter. The night was over as far as I was concerned and looking after my brother seemed a suitable ending to it.

'Where is he?' I asked Jason, jiggling the keys from hand to hand.

'He's in the men's toilet.'

Hugh was already gone, excusing his way through the crowd. He emerged with a talkative Grant draped around his shoulders.

'Yes, OK, Grant, mate, I hear you.

Come on, let's go.'

Of course, I had no idea where the family car was parked and I didn't think my brother would be able to remember.

'Press the remote on the key,' Hugh suggested as we stood on the doorstep and faced the paddock of locked vehicles.

Out in the pre-dawn darkness, lights flashed in answer. Nothing was said as we covered the distance to the car, Grant having lapsed into silence. There wasn't anything I wanted to say and, by the sound of his breathing, Hugh had little enough spare energy for talking.

He propped his passive burden against the car while I opened the back passenger door.

With Grant settled in the back seat and already asleep, I had no reason to delay. I gathered my skirt around me, eased myself behind the wheel and turned the ignition key.

Hugh bent down and leaned on the window-frame so that our eyes met in the light from the instrument panel.

'Drive carefully,' he said.

'Goodbye,' I replied, somewhat mournfully, and I meant it, if only he knew.

★ ★ ★

It was Grant who brought me the note days later. I was in the sheds doing rainy-day maintenance when he returned from the township.

'From Hugh,' he muttered, the matter of his secret association with a Trevellyn still a sore point between us.

'What has he to say?'

'I'm just the messenger. If you want to know, why don't you open it?'

He stood in the doorway for a moment, gloomily surveying the rain, before splashing across the yard to the house.

The handwriting was firm and bold, as I would've expected, the message brief and to the point.

*Now I've found you, we need to talk.
I'll be at Long Hollow tomorrow at
dusk.*

Hugh.

I re-folded the note and carefully
placed it in the hip pocket of my jeans,
as if it was precious, as if it was
important, as if I needed it for
reference. As if! Whom was I fooling? I
already knew it by heart.

So Hugh had worked out who had
disturbed his sleep the night Tirra Lirra
sheep had been stolen. But what could
I tell him that he didn't already know?
The sheep were gone.

I was aware of Hugh's note in my
pocket all through dinner. I wondered
what he would do if I didn't turn up
— wait there as it grew darker and
darker and finally realise I wasn't
coming? To me that seemed unkind.
Just how to let him know was the
sticking point. Perhaps I could write
back, pointing out the impossibility of
the situation.

That wasn't a good idea. It could be days before the mail went out to Tirra Lirra and that wouldn't solve the problem of him waiting in vain for me. I thought of calling him on his mobile but, of course, I didn't know the number. And since I'd lost mine in the river how was I to call the homestead from our phone without being overheard? Impossible.

I couldn't ask Grant to do it for me after making such a fuss over his secret relationship with Hugh. The two may have been friends in America but that friendship couldn't continue back home, not with Dad and Grandmother Frazer keeping alive the feud between our families.

The feud! It was such an accepted part of our lives I'd never thought to question it before. We had nothing to do with the Trevellyns. Now I wanted to know what it was all about. I couldn't ask Dad, not without upsetting him. I wondered if Grandmother Frazer would tell me and just as quickly dismissed the idea. My stern grandmother didn't encourage the exchange of intimacies.

I needn't have worried about Hugh Trevellyn keeping a lonely vigil at Long Hollow. When I got there the next evening, the Reserve was deserted. I turned off the parking lights and stepped out of the truck. Only a flutter of wings, the splash of homing water birds landing on the still surface of the billabong broke the darkening silence.

If this was some joke of Grant's, a payback, I didn't think much of it. After a night of indecision I'd decided I owed Hugh the courtesy of telling him, face to face, that I couldn't help. I had no further information.

Face to face! I hadn't realised how nervous that made me. There was no reason to be nervous. Meeting with a Trevellyn didn't frighten me, and my father thought I was miles away, in the township. So what was the problem?

A shadow moved out of the corner where I'd discovered the evidence of the sheep stealing. Was it a stray beast, or a kangaroo? It wasn't until it loomed up close that I could see it was Hugh.

'Hope I didn't alarm you,' he said. 'Had to leave the truck back at the last gully. It's a bit boggy after yesterday's rain.'

'I expected you to come by the forest road, and was looking for your lights,' I babbled, a little short of breath. 'Look, Hugh, I only came to tell you I couldn't come ...'

He was smiling, amusement causing crinkles around his eyes, but he said nothing, letting me rabbit on.

'And there isn't much I can tell you about the sheep stealing, only what I told you on the phone, that they were there.'

He had a really wonderful laugh. It made me forget to be nervous and laugh with him.

'Well, you know what I mean,' I finished, lamely.

'As a matter of fact, I do, but you'll have to give me a better reason than that.'

'A better reason for what?'

I shouldn't have asked. He stepped up to face me, and grasped my shoulders.

'For coming. I think you came because we were interrupted the night of the muster. Isn't that the truth?'

Perhaps I'm slow on the uptake, but he was kissing me before I could deny it, and I was liking being kissed! Then I remembered the purpose of our meeting.

Reluctantly, I pulled away.

Hugh made no attempt to hold me against my will, but moved to stand between me and the truck, a half-smile on his lips, as if he knew I had escape in mind — and why. Could it have been he was enjoying himself?

'Well, since I'm here, perhaps I should tell you what I saw the night your sheep were stolen. I don't usually come home this way because my father objects to me being anywhere near Tirra Lirra, because of the feud between our families,' I explained, seeing the puzzled look on his face.

'Oh,' was all he said, dismissing that with a shrug. 'Then why didn't he veto your telephone call?'

'He did.'

'And you went against his orders to warn me?'

I wished Hugh hadn't reminded me of that. It only made me feel bad about this secret meeting. I hated deceiving my father.

'Well, I felt I couldn't let that happen to anyone,' I mumbled.

A night wind had sprung up, cutting through my light jacket.

'Look, why don't we get in the truck, out of the cold?'

And make it more awkward for you to kiss me, I thought. I had to do something to boost my willpower. But as soon as I'd made the suggestion I wished I hadn't. There was a likelihood he would see through my subterfuge and laugh at me, again. But inside the truck, he became reflective.

'And I took no notice of your

warning,' he mused, as if our getting into the vehicle was no interruption.

I seized on the confession.

'Why was that? Because I was a female and you didn't believe me?'

'No, not really. I thought I knew better.'

He turned in the seat and faced me.

'To my regret, I must say.'

I wanted to make him feel better.

'You probably couldn't have made it here in time, anyway,' I suggested. 'It was a good while after I'd seen the truck that I rang you.'

'It wasn't until the next morning that I had second thoughts.'

'Were you coming to check it out when you saw me in the river?'

'Yes.' He grinned. 'And a good thing I did, eh?'

I had to agree. What might have happened to me if he hadn't come didn't bear thinking about.

Wanting to talk about something other than that close call, I asked, 'But what could you have done if you had believed me?'

'We probably could've arranged road blocks. There wouldn't be too many loaded transport trucks coming through the forest at that time of night. No, I blew it.'

There was very little I could say when he was being so brutally honest with himself. I thought of Jason being called out in the middle of the night and the distance he'd have had to travel.

'But would the police have been able to get here in time?'

'Probably not, but Dad and I would have followed them to either the sale yards or the abbatoirs, or at least taken their registration number. Our vehicles would've been faster than their loaded truck.'

We were silent for a few minutes, each lost in our own thoughts, Hugh with his regrets, probably, and me with a dilemma. Should I ask any more questions or leave right now before I got involved? My curiosity got the better of me, as it always did.

'Have you any idea who they could have been?'

'No, I've even forgotten the name Jason gave when he asked for information on their behalf.'

I frowned.

'Whatever the name, it seems strange that they went to the police station.'

'Or clever.'

Sitting with Hugh in the warmth of the truck cabin, I suddenly became aware of the almost magnetic appeal of the strong body beside me. I lost all interest in sheep stealing, my curiosity piqued by the man himself.

Was he right? Was my being here in Long Hollow less to do with the right thing and more about the attraction of him? For a moment, I allowed myself to remember the pleasure of his kisses.

'Hello, are you with me?'

Hugh's voice interrupted my reverie. He waved a hand in front of my eyes.

'Sorry, what do you mean, clever?' I stammered, glad of the darkness that covered the flush sweeping up my neck.

'Ah, so you were listening. Well, don't you think that was a clever ploy involving the police, making sure no questions were asked?'

'Yes, but wasn't there the risk that it would invite friendly concern and perhaps a visit from the landowner?'

'But not until morning, surely.'

I was fast losing interest again. I had contributed the little I knew. What I needed to do now was to take my regrets and go home to Balool, away from this disturbing influence. It was as if Hugh read my mind.

'What are we going to do about us?' he asked, leaning slightly toward me.

I became flustered. Whatever was wrong with me? Anyone would think I'd never been asked that kind of a question before, or one very much like it in blunter terms.

I tried to think of a witty reply, to show him I was cool, but my brain wasn't working that way. It was urging my body forward to meet his in the narrow confines of the cabin. He reached up and turned on the interior light.

'I want to look at you,' he said, gently tracing the contours of my face, and framing it with callous-free hands.

'What are we going to do?' I repeated idiotically, mesmerised by the intent in his eyes.

Kiss me, my heart clamoured. Again, uncannily, Hugh read my mind.

If I thought getting into the cabin of the truck would prove a barrier to our growing attraction, I was wrong. There was nothing awkward about the way I melted into his embrace.

After the first urgent kiss, he lifted his head and murmured, 'Well, that question has been answered.'

I lost all sense of time after that until a sharp shower buffeted the vehicle, startling me back into the everyday world. I sat up straight, suddenly conscious of my mussed-up state.

'I'll be late for dinner,' I said, inanely,

fussing around for my hair-band.

Finding it, I pulled down the visor for the mirror I kept hidden there. In the poor light, the reflected face was not familiar to me. I had never seen such womanly softness, the lips swollen, all traces of lipstick kissed away.

I gave up on tying back my hair, and turned to look at the man who had brought about this change in me.

'I can't leave just yet.' He grinned, indicating the weather, and reached for me again.

The rain beat a loud tattoo on the cab roof, like his strong heartbeat under my hand. I wanted to know more about Hugh but only clichés came into my head. How could I ask where had he been all my life?

As if he knew, he began to talk about himself. His story was no different to that of many children isolated by distance. A happy childhood, lessons by correspondence, shared with an older brother, then boarding school in the city from an early age.

'Where is your brother?' I asked.

'He is working with the World Health Organisation in Africa.'

Questions were forming in my mind. 'So what were you doing at Harvard? Shouldn't you have come home to take over running the property?'

The arms around me tightened imperceptively.

'I have,' he said.

I sat up to get a better look at his face.

'Both my father's sons showed little aptitude for the nitty-gritty of farming, but we were allowed the education best suited to our talents. In my brother's case, that was medicine and in mine, business administration. Property management is much more involved than ever before, plus, with computers, business can be conducted from anywhere. So, here I am, back home,' he finished.

I felt ridiculously pleased about that. Hugh held me away from himself.

'Now, what about you? Why are you

still here and not pursuing a career in the city?'

The rain had passed. It was quite dark outside. A sudden thought crossed my mind. How would he find his way back to his vehicle?

'Why do I get the feeling I'm not wanted?' he quipped when I asked him. 'There's a real touch of the here's your hat and there's the door about that.'

He put a hand in one of the many pockets of his coat and, with a spontaneous laugh, produced a torch.

'I was thinking of a famous Mae West saying,' he explained, still smiling but choosing not to enlighten me.

There was nothing frivolous about the long, hard kiss he gave me before he opened the door and was gone. I darkened the cabin, wiped the fogged window and watched the progress of the bobbing circle of light until it disappeared in the trees.

I didn't remember much about the drive home, only realising when I got into the kitchen at Balool just how cold I was, and how hungry.

'This curry smells great, Mum,' I said, seeking the warmth of the Aga and lifting the lid of the cast-iron pot simmering gently on its hotplate.

'I can put the rice on, now you've arrived.'

My mother busied herself beside me.

'As you go past to your room, will you tell your father and Grant it'll only be fifteen minutes? Oh, and take your clean clothes with you,' she added, picking up a pile of neatly-ironed laundry and thrusting it into my arms. 'Your grandmother washed, despite the weather.'

My mother was obviously cross about what was to her the unnecessary use of the generator for the clothes drier, especially for slow-drying jeans. Jeans! Instinctively, I put a hand to my hip pocket. It was empty. Too late, I realised Hugh's letter had been left in my other jeans when I changed to go to Long Hollow. Suddenly, I felt cold again. Did they know I'd been with a Trevellyn?

Grandmother Frazer continued with her task of setting out the cutlery on the table.

'Grandmother Frazer,' I began, my stomach muscles tightening.

She wasn't going to help me, crossing the room to bring condiments from the cupboard, her lips thin with annoyance. It entered my head that something would have to be done to resolve the tension between the two women, but not now. A larger battle was threatening, between the whole household and me, and the thought of it was playing havoc with my nervous system.

Oh, what a can of worms I'd opened up by disobeying my father! I willed myself to be calm and tried again.

'Grandmother Frazer, did I leave . . . was there a letter in the pocket of my jeans?'

My mother, ready to criticise every move her mother-in-law made, saw an opportunity.

'There, I knew you shouldn't wash anything of Lyndal's unless she put it out.'

Now that the table had been arranged according to her satisfaction, my grandmother dug into her apron pocket, brought out Hugh's letter, and handed it to me without a word.

'Was it important, Lyndal?' my mother asked over her shoulder, suddenly busy with cooking the rice.

I looked at my grandmother. She stared back. Had she read the letter? I didn't understand her well enough to judge if she was capable of that.

'No, Mum, it wasn't important.'

4

It was the next afternoon before I had a chance to talk alone with my grandmother. I found her in the front garden giving a late prune to the neglected bush roses.

'You shouldn't get upset with my mother,' I began. 'It's not like her to be rude but she's so stressed out with overwork and worry about Dad.'

'I know that, Lyndal, and am making allowances.'

Making allowances? I almost choked.

'Are you making allowances for me, too?' I demanded recklessly, stung by the unfair criticism of my mother.

'I don't have to, do I?'

I was surprised by the warmth in her voice. Did that mean she hadn't read Hugh's letter? I took a gamble that her strict standards of behaviour wouldn't allow her to do such a thing, and lied.

'Of course not.'

She stopped her pruning and looked straight at me.

'But that letter was something you wanted to keep secret, wasn't it?'

'Why would you think that, Grandmother Frazer?' I asked, a little sorry I'd begun the conversation.

'I wish you'd call me something other than that ridiculous mouthful,' she retorted sharply, expertly removing a dead cane and dropping it on the pile of prunings. 'It was useful only when Clarice's mother was alive and you children needed to distinguish between your two grandmothers.'

'What would you like me to call you?' I asked, quite forgetting the matter of the letter.

She turned away from the roses, closed and secured the secateurs and removed the protective gardening gloves she wore.

'Perhaps just Grandmama would be sufficient,' she said mildly, sitting down on a nearby garden seat.

I joined her and got back to the task of building bridges between her and my mother.

'About Mum being difficult. What I'm trying to say is she doesn't really mean to be so cranky.'

My grandmother's austere face softened a little.

'I had wanted to be a help to her, but I feel nothing but a hindrance.'

'But you are a help,' I insisted. 'Perhaps not in the way you intended but the difference in Dad since you came is noticeable, which is good for Mum.'

That seemed to please her.

'It must be close to afternoon tea-time,' I suggested, standing up and gathering the secateurs and gloves.

She didn't move, so I sat down again.

'You haven't answered my question. The letter in your jeans pocket is secret, isn't it, Lyndal?' she asked. 'What are you keeping from your mother?'

'It's nothing, Grandmother — Grandmama,' I bluffed, my tongue stumbling over the unfamiliar name. 'Just a note from one of my friends. Nothing important.'

'You're not very good at lying, are you?'

I was going to continue with the lie but there was something in the faded blue eyes behind their glasses that I hadn't noticed before — kindliness. Suddenly, I wanted to tell her the truth.

'No, I'm not. I've been told my face gives everything away,' I admitted shamefacedly. 'Grant says I'd be hopeless as a poker player.'

Some of the softness went out of Grandmama's face at the mention of card playing. She wasn't about to change her stand on gambling.

'Not that I play poker,' I hastened to add. 'It's just what he says.'

'So, are you going to tell me with what the letter was concerned and why you should want to keep it from your parents?'

She had no idea how much I wanted to talk about it, or at least, about its writer. I suppose it was natural enough to want a confidante, to share with someone the mixed feelings Hugh was causing me. I hadn't dared ring Louise on our home phone in case I was overheard, and it was days before netball practice would take me to the township again. I regretted not having replaced my lost mobile phone.

Could I confide in Grandmama? Despite the glimpse of a softer side to her nature she was still a Frazer. They had long memories.

The question remained unanswered. The familiar white car with the chequered stripe was coming up the long driveway, just as the afternoon-tea gong sounded across the garden.

'You timed that right, Jason,' I joked to the tall figure in the blue uniform who came to walk inside with Grand-mama and me.

'Timing is what good policing is all about.'

He laughed, holding open the door. I hurried away to help my mother with serving, relieved that the matter of Hugh's letter had been overtaken by events.

When I carried in the tea-tray, the living-room looked crowded, like it had in the old days, before my father's illness. Dad sat in his usual chair by the fire, his mother opposite him.

Grant had come in from the office together with Ray, the head stockman. Jason rose from his chair to take the tray out of my hands and set it down. Mum began pouring the tea.

It was Grant who brought the conversation around to sheep stealing by asking Jason for an update on the thefts.

'Fortunately, there haven't been any since the Trevellyn incident,' he answered. 'We're continuing with our enquiries.'

The name of Trevellyn shattered the illusion of a pleasant gathering for some of us. My father's face was a thunder-cloud. I wondered if he remembered the night I had wanted to ring our neighbour and warn him. I looked to Grandmama. All the softness I'd seen in the garden was gone from her face.

My mouth went dry as I realised how close I'd come to confiding in her. It wouldn't have been a good thing. Obviously the feud was still very much alive for her, too.

Not for the first time, I wondered whatever it was that had caused such enmity.

'Two hundred was a lot of sheep to lose in one night,' Grant said. 'So, that means it was pretty well organised, not some two-bit, small-time operation. We're talking about a big truck.'

'It was a double-decker,' I offered, without thinking.

Suddenly, all eyes were on me, that is, all except Dad's. He was glaring into the flames. I needed to explain, but I had to be careful. Only he and I knew I'd seen the transport truck, and to his knowledge, done nothing about it.

'Dual-tyre tracks.'

No-one spoke, waiting.

'I was doing a regular boundary-fence check one day, and I saw where the truck had backed up against the fence.'

My explanation sounded unsatisfactory even to my ears.

'We were lucky our sheep weren't in a paddock close to the road,' I went on. 'They could just as easily have been taken.'

As the hostess, my mother wasn't going to allow the awkwardness to continue a minute longer.

'Another cup, anyone? Alec?' she enquired, rising to replenish the tea-pot.

At that moment, the telephone rang. She continued to the kitchen to answer on the extension. All I could hear was the murmur of her voice.

Jason came to stand beside my chair. 'You didn't tell me you knew anything about the sheep being stolen from Tirra Lirra,' he said.

I felt the beginnings of a flush.

'There was nothing to tell you,' I replied, which wasn't really a lie.

Any telling was between Hugh and me. I met Jason's direct gaze, willing myself to remain calm, and appear guileless.

'It's the talk of the district, you know.'

My mother chose that moment to appear in the doorway.

'It's for you, Lyndal.'

'Oh, that'll be Louise, with details of the Netball Association's regional meeting,' I exclaimed with relief, getting to my feet. 'We're delegates.'

'No, dear, it isn't Louise, it's a man. He gave his name as Hugh.'

The room became silent again, with all eyes focused on me. Dismayed, I looked around at the faces, first to my mother, who was interested only in delivering the correct message before returning to the kitchen. To my father the name meant nothing, but Grandmama's eyes had narrowed. My doubts about her reading Hugh's letter resurfaced for a split second. Jason and the head stockman seemed oblivious to the tension.

Behind me, Grant spoke.

'Ah, I'll look after that, Mum.'

Her bewildered look made him explain.

'I ordered some salt-licks for the cattle, and told the salesman to talk to Lyndal about delivery dates. After all, that's her business. Mine is doing the ordering and signing the cheques. Something might've changed, the price gone up or supply been delayed.'

He strode past me.

'I'll take it in the office.'

Every fibre of my being wanted to follow him but Jason had begun his farewells.

'This doesn't get the work done, does it?' he said, shaking my father's hand and bending with a goodbye smile for Grandmama.

There was nothing I could do but accompany him to the police car, my mind reeling.

What madness had made Hugh ring Balool, and what could he want?

Distracted by my thoughts, I was caught unawares when Jason stopped suddenly and turned to gaze down into my face.

'You're looking particularly pretty in that dress,' he said. 'The colour suits you.'

Before I could stammer a perfunctory thank-you, he bent and kissed me hard on the lips. It was the first time he'd done that and I was surprised. I stood there, looking silly, I suppose, as he got into the car and rolled down the window.

'You'd tell me if you saw anything suspicious, wouldn't you?'

It was more of an order than a question. Uneasily, I began to wonder if he suspected me. I nodded, my face creasing into a stiff smile. As soon as the police car disappeared, I stormed around the veranda into the office. Thankfully, Grant was alone.

'Whatever was Hugh thinking of,

ringing here and giving his name?' I demanded.

My brother leaned back in his chair, tilting it dangerously, and grinned at me.

'Obviously he was thinking of you, little sister.'

'Well, if he was he'd have known it was a no-no,' I retorted, flattered, in spite of myself.

'No isn't a word he recognises, and no-no is definitely like a red rag to a bull,' Grant said, straightening up to deliver the coup-de-grace. 'He's coming over.'

My brother could be very annoying at times. His grin widened as he watched me grapple with the disastrous news.

'Coming over? He can't! Whatever does he want to do that for? Why didn't you stop him?'

Grant was obviously enjoying himself.

'Could I stop night following day?'

His laugh followed me as I left the

office and strode back along the veranda in the direction of the sheds and the motorbike. Hugh had to be stopped.

For once, the bike responded immediately to my kick-start, and I reached the front entrance to Balool in record time. There was no sign of Hugh. I parked in amongst the trees on the roadside, well out of sight of the homestead, my pulse racing at the thought of preventing a major calamity. Well, that's what I told myself and I had no reason to question my motives any further.

As I waited, it began to rain lightly. Exasperated, I wished the wet weather was over, and we could have more than one fine day in a row. Even a drought would be welcome right now. Buttoning up my coat under my chin, I pulled my cap down farther around my ears and sought the shelter of the largest gum tree, my temper fraying rapidly.

It seemed an age before the utility truck from Tirra Lirra splashed its way along the road and pulled up. I wrenched open the off-side door and got in.

'What particular madness are you suffering from?' I demanded.

'And hello to you, too,' Hugh replied laconically, leaning over to remove my cap and toss it on to the shelf behind him.

He ruffled my hair, his fingers tightening to draw my wet face closer to his bent head.

Did he think a kiss was going to solve this problem? It only made it worse. I tried to beat him off, my fists thumping against the solid wall of his chest, futilely.

An arm sneaked around my body, entrapping my outrage and quietening me.

'Why are you doing this?' I mumbled weakly, making one last effort to resist.

'Because I like kissing you.' He laughed against my mouth. 'And because you like it, too.'

Hugh was right. I did like it. For a

brief moment I thought of Jason's kiss. It certainly hadn't packed a punch like this. I melted, and lost track of time.

'Now, what was all that about?' Hugh asked, at last.

I had to think for a while before I could remember my original question.

'Whatever are you doing over here?'

'Coming to see you, of course,' he replied.

'In spite of the feud between our families?'

I could hear the note of anxiety creeping back into my voice. Hugh put a finger under my chin, lifting my face so that I was looking directly into his eyes.

'You really don't think I'm going to let anything stand between us, do you?'

The declaration thrilled me but at the same time frightened me.

'Do I have to spell it out? My father is ill. The very name of Trevellyn is enough to bring on a seizure. How do you think my family will react to you and me . . .'

The words died in my throat. What exactly were we doing? Just kissing. Surely there was no law against that. Lots of people did it. But, even as I clutched at this piece of illogical reasoning, I knew what was between Hugh and me was serious. I'd fought off that certainty since the first time I looked into his eyes, not knowing who he was. I'd told myself then it was gratitude at being saved from near drowning. Now I knew better.

But how could I give him up?

The very thought triggered tears that trembled on my eyelashes. I put up a hand to flick them away.

'Hey, hey, what's this?' Hugh cajoled, capturing my hand.

The tenderness of his touch only made it worse. The welling tears became a trickle.

'Don't you understand? It means I can't see you any more,' I gulped.

He searched his pockets until he found a handkerchief, gave it a rueful look before wiping my face. It smelled strongly of diesel oil.

'This feud you say exists between our families, what is it about?' he asked.

'I don't know, but it's always been there, yet never as bad as it is now,' I replied.

'Well, you'd better find out, hadn't you? Perhaps we can do something about it. As I said, nothing is going to come between us.'

I laid my head against his chest, worrying about how to do what he suggested. Was there a chance my mother would tell me if I asked her? For a brief moment, I wondered why of all the people to come into my life right now it had to be a Trevellyn. But I couldn't wish it hadn't happened.

I knew I should be strong but decided it was all too hard. It was much easier to burrow into Hugh's neck, feeling his arms tighten around me as I did.

Our quiet moment only lasted a minute. The problem wouldn't go away. I sat up, distancing myself from him, a question forming in my mind.

'You act as if you've never heard of the feud, that I'm making it all up, exaggerating, though why you should think that is a mystery.'

He shook his head slowly from side to side.

'Lyndal, Lyndal, you've got me all wrong. I'm not saying that. It just isn't mentioned at home.'

Was that possible? Hardly. They say it takes two to tango. Well, it certainly takes more than one person to carry on a feud.

'You could ask your parents,' I challenged him.

He put up his hands in mock surrender and laughed.

'OK, OK.'

I could see I was being humoured, that he didn't believe me. Until he did there was the risk he'd confront my father. He'd said nothing would stand between us. I took that to mean no-one, too.

Suddenly, I could see a way to make

him take me seriously. I would get his promise.

'And until my father is better, I suggest you stay away from Balool.'

No longer laughing, he looked at me for a long time before he answered.

'As I said, what is between us is something very special. If it makes you happy, I'll respect your wishes. You leave me no choice but to stay away from Balool.'

If I was being honest I had to admit I was disappointed. I expected him to object, to refuse, to fight me on this, not give in so easily. Perhaps he didn't really mean what he said, and this wasn't something special after all.

'Then it's agreed? No visits, no letters, no phone calls?'

He nodded.

'It's for the best,' I added hopefully, giving him one last chance to object.

He nodded again.

'Good,' I said, opening the door and getting out.

The Netball Association Special Meeting was being held in a resort-style convention complex on the outskirts of the rural city. The group of single-storey bungalows clustered around a taller building looked particularly inviting after the long drive.

'I hope there's a heated swimming-pool,' Louise said, shivering as we left the air-conditioned car to register in the main building.

'Yes, we wouldn't want to have brought along our swimmers for nothing,' I replied, my eyes taking in the charming décor of the lobby. 'It seems a long time since summer.'

I studied the list of amenities.

'Looks like we're in luck.'

We were pleased with our accommodation, too. The windows of our unit looked out on to a private garden.

'I'm going to enjoy this break,' I announced, unpacking my bag and generally spreading myself around.

'We have work to do,' Louise reminded me. 'This business of banning pregnant players from matches doesn't affect us personally.'

'Speak for yourself,' I interrupted. 'Somewhere down the track I hope to be married and pregnant and still be playing netball.'

'But it will be disastrous for small clubs like ours,' she went on, ignoring my remarks. 'It'd be hard to stay in the competition if all our married girls became pregnant at the same time.'

I could think of several cheeky things to say in reply but decided it was more diplomatic to leave them unsaid.

'Yes, yes, Lou, I know. It's all about increased public liability insurance and the fear of being sued if something happened to a player or her baby.'

What I'd been referring to was how good it was to be able to get away from Balool and forget everything for a couple of days, and by everything I meant more than the situation at home. That had become a lot easier now the workload was being shared by Grant. It allowed me to take these few days off. No, what I really wanted to forget was the dilemma of my relationship with Hugh.

Louise and I had had plenty of time to talk it over during the long drive to Wagga Wagga, but I still wasn't sure of my feelings, or of his. He had accepted my demands so readily it made me wonder if he was sincere.

'He sounds a really great guy,' Louise said. 'I wouldn't mind meeting him if you're not interested.'

'I didn't say I wasn't interested,' I retorted, a little too sharply for a friend.

'Sorry.'

'It's just the situation at home, and he did give up easily.'

There didn't seem much more to say after that and we changed to talking about making time for some shopping.

'It's late-closing night. What are you looking for?'

I remembered that now. Gathering up my jacket and bag, I stood expectantly by the door. Louise took the hint and joined me, the duties of a delegate shelved until tomorrow.

★　★　★

The talk amongst the delegates in the resort dining-room was animated, and certainly not about the serious discussions of the day. The chattering was at its loudest when suddenly, of one accord, the female voices became silent. The soft background music and tinkling of the water feature filled the vacuum as all eyes turned in the direction of the entrance.

'What is it?' I asked Louise, who was facing that way and had a better view of the room.

'A good-looking guy has just come in,' she answered, unconsciously straightening up.

The look on her face made me swivel in my chair to see for myself. The last person I expected to see was following the dining-room hostess through the tables towards us. He seemed unaware of the stir he was causing in the all-female gathering.

'Hugh!' I breathed, turning back to face her, at once dumbfounded, pleased but not pleased.

He certainly knew how to make things hard for me, and so did my brother. I could imagine him back at Balool, chortling at his cleverness in divulging my whereabouts to his friend.

Louise was suitably impressed.

'That's Hugh?'

There was no time to answer her. The two had reached our table. For a long moment Hugh and I stared at each other. The hostess, all smiles, bustled between us and the waiters' station, setting another place at our two-person table. Thanking her, Hugh pulled up a chair from nearby, and joined Louise and myself.

The diners returned to their meals, but I was well aware of the furtive looks in our direction. I wasn't used to being at the centre of attention from strangers. A familiar flush crept up my neck. I couldn't stop it.

I leaned forward to hiss, 'What are you doing here? You promised!'

'You didn't say no chance meetings.'

He grinned widely, pleased with himself. It was all I could do not to show how pleased I was, too. I scowled. I had to. He was right, but I wasn't about to admit it. He had embarrassed me.

'Because it never occurred to me this would happen,' I explained.

Hugh knew we were both glad to see each other. He dismissed my pathetic excuse with a deepening of his grin and a faint shrug of his broad shoulders.

He turned to Louise.

'Hello, you must be Louise,' he said, sending the colour racing into her face, too.

What two unsophisticated country girls we must have seemed!

The introductions over, Hugh made a suggestion.

'When you've finished your meal, why don't the three of us go dancing?'

5

For days after my return to Balool, I rode an emotional roller-coaster, one moment high on the knowledge that Hugh loved me, then suddenly swooping down into the depths of despair over our future, or rather, the lack of one.

Hugh couldn't have been totally happy, either. The snatched evening in Wagga had a bitter-sweet ending. On our return to the conference centre, we found the television room deserted. Louise excused herself after a last coffee from the self-service bar and he and I settled on the comfortable lounge before a dying fire.

It wasn't the most romantic of places to hear a declaration of love, with the likelihood of a night-owl guest barging in on us, but that was what happened.

We'd been quiet for a while when Hugh spoke.

'You realise this is for real, don't you, Lyn? I love you. We belong together.'

'That sounds almost like a proposal,' I remarked contentedly, without lifting my head from his shoulder.

The late hour, the dimly-lit room, the flickering flames as the logs stirred and collapsed, the luxury of being in Hugh's arms, all created a dream-like atmosphere.

'If it was, would you accept?' His voice was a loving murmur above me.

'Of course, but with a proviso. You'd have to wait.'

'Wait? While you hit the shops again for a wedding outfit? How long?'

'Until my father is better.'

I could feel his body stiffen.

'You can't mean that!' he demanded.

I sat up then, my heart turning over at the angry look on his face.

'But, Hugh, I told you.'

I went over what I thought we'd already agreed upon. Remembering now how we'd parted with a frostiness between us, my spirits plummeted yet again.

My mother, much less frazzled these days with Grant at home, must've noticed my mood changes since the conference. She quietly came up to me as I kneeled in the vegetable garden, pulling carrots for the kitchen.

'Everything all right with you, Lyndal?'

I started, not with fright, but at the question itself. Did she have any idea of what was wrong with me? Had I given myself away? But how? I knew she couldn't have found Hugh's letter. I carried it with me at all times, the much-folded notepaper now worn at the edges from many readings. No, she couldn't know, not unless Grandmama had voiced her suspicions. I dismissed that as unlikely, given the state of their relationship.

But was it possible to answer my mother's question without confessing to the secret meetings between myself and a member of the despised Trevellyn family, and the promise I'd made him? I didn't think so.

I looked hard into the steady eyes that held mine.

'You know you can trust me,' she said.

I would have agreed that was true about most things, but even if my mother didn't share my father's strong feelings on the subject, wouldn't her knowing my secret place too much of a strain on her loyalties?

Suddenly, the desire to learn more about the feud that was keeping Hugh and me apart overcame my fears. Perhaps I could ask without telling her about him, if I was careful.

'What caused the feud between the Frazers and the Trevellyns? I can't remember ever being told.'

My mother was genuinely surprised.

'Goodness, Lyndal, why are you bothering yourself about that now? You're as bad as your father. As I tell him, it belongs in the past.'

Once the subject had been broached without causing an adverse reaction, questions were rushing to my lips.

'If it belongs in the past, why is Dad still so angry? Was it something that happened between him and Mr Trevellyn? Did they get into a fight? What about? Why weren't we told?'

She glanced back towards the house before answering.

'You weren't told because you never wanted to know. And it was a long time ago,' she said.

'In Grandmama's time or before?'

My mother was obviously reluctant to talk about whatever it was. She took the carrots out of my hand.

'Your grandmother and your father are both resting just now. Come and help me make this carrot cake whilst I tell you as much as I can.'

She led the way from the garden. I couldn't understand the need for secrecy and said so.

'Why weren't Grant and I told?' Remembered childhood resentment of always being fobbed off as too young made me ask, 'Or does he know and I don't?'

Before answering, my mother crossed the kitchen and carefully closed the door that led to the rest of the house.

'No, Lyndal, he didn't ever ask either. It's never been a secret really but I didn't encourage talk about it when you two were younger, hoping it would be forgotten by this generation at least. It seems that was expecting too much. They had to bring it up again.'

She emphasised her impatience with her husband and his mother by slamming the heavy mixing bowl down on the table so hard the scales rattled.

'When I came here as a bride I could've done with the company of a woman neighbour,' she added, almost to herself.

I couldn't believe my ears. A feud carried on into the next generation? It must've been something terrible. My mind, already fixated on romance, came up with an immediate scenario. Perhaps a Trevellyn stole a Frazer woman at the altar, or vice versa. That could cause bad feelings that festered over the years, especially if they lived nearby.

The whirring of the electric vegetable chopper masked my mother's gentle voice. I could only hear snatches of what she was saying.

' . . . settled in the mid-eighteen-eighties . . . usual skirmishes over fences but nothing . . . '

The noise stopped.

'The Trevellyns prospered, some said through shady deals. Hugh Trevellyn eventually became very influential.'

My eyes flew wide open at the name, although I knew my mother wasn't referring to my Hugh. This feud began before he, or I, was born, I knew that, and a feud over resented success, not even something as important as a broken love affair. That couldn't be right. The way my father carried on, you'd think it all happened only yesterday, and the present Trevellyns were responsible. It was hard to keep the incredulity out of my voice. It rose to another pitch.

'Is that all?' I almost shrieked.

'Shush,' my mother urged with an anxious glance towards the door to the passageway. 'You'll disturb your father.'

With competent hands, she added the flour and emptied the mixture into the cake tin, tapped the air bubbles out and popped it into the pre-heated oven. I sat open-mouthed whilst the preparation utensils were whisked away into the sink and the kettle brought to the boil. Only then did she go on.

'Old Hugh Trevellyn . . . '

'Did I hear the sound of cups and saucers?' a voice from the doorway asked.

My mother broke off her story, gave me an I-told-you-so look and hurried forward to assist her husband on to a kitchen chair.

'Am I too early for a piece of cake?'

'Much too early,' his wife replied. 'Carrot cake is always better the next day, when it's iced, you know that.

Could I interest you in a slice of boiled fruit cake instead?'

Frustrated by the interruption which I obviously had brought on myself, I sat fiddling with my teaspoon, only half-hearing the conversation across the table, my mind occupied with the disjointed story and wishing for more details.

There was little hope of that now. My mother wouldn't risk upsetting her husband. It was clear the subject had to be dropped for the time being.

6

Jason, casually dressed in off-duty jeans and driving his own car, arrived early one morning while we were still at breakfast. After greeting the family and accepting a cup of coffee he gave the reason for his visit.

'I thought I'd go on your rounds with you, if that's OK,' he said to me. 'Should be quite an experience for a city guy.'

It was the last thing I expected. He had shown little interest in me since he kissed me. Of course, that could've been because I saw to it we were never alone, but he hadn't tried very hard to change that.

I must have looked surprised, caught out, my mind elsewhere as it often was lately. Not that all my thinking had done me much good. I was no closer to a way around the problem of my future.

What if Dad didn't get much better? I couldn't bear to think of that. He had to! Nor could I think of Jason Dunstan as a romantic substitute for Hugh.

'Riding pillion,' Jason added, bringing my attention back to his request.

I didn't like the idea of taking him with me. I enjoyed going about my work alone. Stupidly, I couldn't think of a good reason to refuse.

All I could say was, 'What about Rowdy?'

Jason wasn't going to be deterred.

'Couldn't you leave him behind?' he asked.

The family laughed at that.

'You'll never part those two. It's a case of love Lyndal, love her dog,' Grant said, knowing the talk of love in front of Jason would make me uncomfortable.

My father came up with a practical suggestion.

'Rowdy could sit on the petrol tank, Lyndal. It wouldn't be the first time. Don't you remember when you and I used to ride together? Rowdy would be up front then.'

He stopped short, the reference to happier times reminding him, and us, of his illness. A silence settled over the breakfast table. My mother, always ready with a diplomatic remark, bridged the awkwardness.

'And you complained loudly about his smell, Alec,' she said.

'Well, working dogs do get a bit whiffy,' my father defended himself.

He was right. After I adjusted to Jason's weight behind me on the motorbike, I called Rowdy to leap up between my arms. As he settled on the petrol tank, the full force of his doggy smell right under my nose completely overpowered the pleasant scent of my companion's distinctive aftershave.

After opening the first gate, Jason got back on behind me, but his hands moved from grasping my shoulders to circling and meeting around my waist. That brought his body closer.

'It's getting bumpier,' he murmured

in my ear by way of explanation. 'I don't fancy being thrown off.'

I could smell his aftershave again.

'What is the name of your after-shave?' I shouted over my shoulder without thinking.

It was a mistake!

'Do you like it?' he asked, his answer bringing his lips perilously close to mine.

'Well, it's decidedly more pleasing than eau de dog,' I said and laughed nervously, turning my head to the front again.

Inside the last gate before Long Hollow, I sent Rowdy off around the scattered mob of sheep, explaining my action to Jason.

'We need to keep the grass eaten down in the paddock beside the road as a fire-break for when summer comes. Since the sheep stealing on Tirra Lirra I haven't been prepared to leave them there overnight.'

'Does that mean you come back out here at the end of the day and round them up?'

'Yes. It's a bother but a necessary precaution,' I replied, idling the engine as I ran my eyes over the paddock, looking for any sick stragglers. 'I wish you'd get on with catching the thieves. It'd be a great help.'

Jason ignored my plea.

'The sheep seem to know where they're going,' he remarked, as the mob streamed through the gate. 'No trouble at all.'

'One case where Rowdy doesn't have much work to do,' I replied. 'They're used to the routine now.'

'So, is it a relatively simple thing to steal sheep?'

'Yes, just back a truck up to a distant boundary fence, well away from the homestead, like out here, and set up a portable yard. With the aid of a half-decent sheepdog that doesn't bark, just nips at their heels, you can load up something that doesn't belong to you.'

I couldn't keep the bitterness out of

my voice. Sheep stealing was the lowest in my book.

A flash of reflected light from the Tirra Lirra side of Long Hollow Reserve caught my attention. I pulled my binoculars from a pocket and trained them in that direction, focusing first on a truck then moving to the three figures working nearby. The powerful lens brought Hugh right beside me. He straightened and turned his head towards me, as if aware of my scrutiny.

I smiled involuntarily, quite forgetting my companion, and my father, and the mysterious feud that was keeping us apart.

'What do you see?' Jason asked.

'Oh, it's one of the Tirra Lirra trucks and workmen mending the fence. Can't see who it is. These binoculars aren't very strong,' I lied, my heart heavy at the thought that if things were different Hugh and I could've met.

Reluctantly, I whistled to Rowdy and when he was back between my arms, I resolutely swung the motorbike away in the opposite direction.

'I'll unlock the gate on to the road and we'll go home that way,' I told Jason, the thought of his arms around my waist again and his body pressed up against mine no longer bearable. 'Not as bumpy for you,' I added, hoping he'd pick up on the hint.

He did. We rode back with his hands decorously on my shoulders.

Grant joined us on our return to the homestead. He waited until Jason drove off before delivering his message.

'I've had a call from Hugh.'

I quickly squashed my delight.

'I wish he wouldn't do that. It makes me nervous. He agreed we wouldn't see each other.'

Grant brushed aside my quibble.

'He didn't ask for you specifically. He wants to talk. He'll meet us at netball practice tonight.'

That really sent me into panic mode. It was almost as bad as coming to Balool although not as life-threatening.

My imagination was running wild as to what the girls in the team would make of his appearance there. Would the gossip get back to Dad? They weren't all as trustworthy as Louise.

'At least he's being more careful about upsetting Dad,' I muttered, grudgingly. 'Just the same, I don't think I should go.'

'Didn't you hear me? He wants to see both of us, says it's important. You'll have to come. We'll take the car. I'll drive.'

'Both of us, did you say? Well, I suppose I should. There's the report on the meeting to give, and I can't afford to miss practice, that's for sure. The team for the country championships hasn't been chosen yet.'

Grant grinned knowingly.

★ ★ ★

I don't think I've ever played so badly. Despite my best efforts, the knowledge that Hugh was waiting shot my concentration to pieces. When the practice was over, the last goodbyes called, I made my way to our car, which Grant had thoughtfully parked in an out-of-the-way corner. No-one was sitting in the passenger seat. My emotions, wound up tight in anticipation all evening, did the usual roller-coaster dip, this time into disappointment.

Just as well Hugh hadn't come, I consoled myself, trying to be reasonable. There was no point in us meeting again, not while Dad was ill. I opened the car door and flopped on to the front seat beside Grant.

'So, you had this drive and long wait all for nothing,' I said.

'Hello, Lyndal,' Hugh's voice came from the back seat.

My heart zoomed upwards. The light from the solitary street lamp touched his serious face as he leaned forward.

'I'm not breaking our agreement,' he assured me. 'There are things we have to talk about.'

Suddenly shy, I looked at my brother.

'In front of Grant?'

'With Grant,' he corrected me. 'He and I have been discussing the sheep stealing that's been going on in the district for the last six months. There's a certain pattern emerging.'

'Is this what they taught you at Harvard? Money well spent, I'd say,' I joked, glad of a chance to release some of my inner tension.

Neither of them laughed as Grant took over the telling.

'We think there's a mastermind behind the thefts. Apart from choosing the right phase of the moon and the weather, they are hitting the right paddocks. Hugh and I think someone is feeding them that information.'

'With one exception,' Hugh said, 'that being Tirra Lirra, the sheep stolen are from properties with daughters . . . '

'And they were all born under the star sign of Aquarius,' I scoffed, unable to take my brother and his friend seriously.

'No, Lyndal, but they were all given

the rush by Jason Dunstan,' Grant said.

I stared at him, unable to believe what he was suggesting, then twisted right round in my seat to face Hugh.

'Is this about jealousy? Do you really think I'm interested in Jason?' I asked.

'I saw you and him over near Long Hollow this morning.'

'Aha! It is jealousy! Well, if you think that will change my mind . . . '

Hugh looked back at me, his gaze steady, neither confirming nor denying the accusation, waiting.

If it wasn't jealousy on his part, could there be any truth in what was being said? If so, it didn't do my ego any good.

'Are you telling me he's been using me to get information?'

'Yes, about the number of sheep in paddocks close to the road. We think he is getting ready to move again, this time on Balool.'

My mouth went dry. Only this morning I had told Jason how easy it was to steal sheep!

'But he's a policeman!' I protested, unwilling to believe I'd been taken in.

'Yes, a very clever policeman,' Hugh remarked, but I hardly heard him.

'I don't believe it,' I announced.

But even as I did, a forgotten remark by Louise weeks ago niggled at my memory. It was when Jason first came to watch netball practice. What had she said? Oh, yes, that Jason had shown an interest in Bobbie Crawford for a time, but there was something else said. Was it about him being kind or helpful? I tried to remember.

'Were sheep stolen from the Crawfords?' I asked.

It was Grant who gave me the answer I already knew.

'We think this morning's ride with you was a prelude to the thieves striking again, tonight,' Hugh said. 'Our plan is to lie in wait for them.'

The shift from suspicion to action was too quick for me.

'Are you sure about this?' I stammered.

Without answering, Grant turned on the ignition, and swung the car in a u-turn, heading in the direction of the road through the forest.

'We think they'll use the gate on the road,' he explained.

'But there's a chain and padlock,' I protested, shot through with guilt.

If they were right and our sheep were in danger, then I was to blame. Not content with telling Jason how easy it was to steal sheep, I'd shown him which gate to access our property from the road. All because I couldn't bear his arms around my waist!

Grant dismissed the locked gate as trifling.

'Nothing a pair of bolt-cutters couldn't handle. No, his biggest trouble will be getting the sheep to move from one paddock to the next at night. But I guess he's figured that out.'

'He'll have helpers,' Hugh said, grimly. 'Experienced helpers.'

Yes, and a good dog that nips at their heels, not a barker, I added silently, sick at heart.

The drive through the forest and out on to the road to Balool seemed to pass more quickly than usual. Little was said, no last-minute planning or attempts made to convince me of Jason's part in the thefts, which was tactful of them both.

Grant parked the car out of sight in the forest, a distance from the gate and, carrying a strong flashlight, led us along the road to a depression formed by recent roadworks.

Huddled in the ditch between him and Hugh, and warmed by their bodies, I listened to their low voices over my head, discussing football scores which were of no interest to me.

How could they be so calm, I asked myself, and what were we doing lying in wait for alleged sheep stealers? I reviewed the so-called evidence against Jason.

In retrospect, I admitted he had spent a lot of time asking questions of my father, but that could be explained.

Talking to Dad probably made life more interesting for a city policeman in a relatively crime-free country posting. It certainly passed the time for the invalid.

If I was taken in by him, I wasn't the only one. Mother certainly made him welcome, too. They couldn't both be fooled, could they? That made me feel a little better.

In fact, I convinced myself Grant and Hugh were wrong. But it didn't matter. Warm and comfortable, I was prepared to humour them for this snatched moment of pleasure. Contented, I slipped in and out of wakefulness.

'Lights coming!'

Hugh's voice, no longer a murmur, cut across my dreamy state. The scudding clouds parted, moonlight momentarily revealing the familiar shape of a stock transporter. So Hugh and Grant were right about Balool being the next target! The vehicle slowed, left the road and came toward us, rattling and bumping over the rough ground.

I automatically ducked farther down, my heart in my mouth, but the truck's headlights were on low beam and not likely to expose our hiding place. Hugh put out a reassuring hand to pat my shoulder. I turned my head to look at him, wishing we were somewhere else, anywhere but here, but his attention was already fixed on the approaching truck.

It reached the gate. The darkly-clad figure of a man got out of the passenger side of the vehicle. He carried something in his hand — the bolt-cutters! Suddenly, the truth of the moment hit me. These people, whoever they were, intended to enter Balool and steal our sheep.

All the months of work and worry since Dad became ill rose in a tidal wave of anger that engulfed me. No-one was going to do that! I leaped up out of our hiding place and sprinted across the uneven ground toward the gate, ignoring the urgent calls from Hugh and Grant.

I launched myself against the would-be thief, screaming and pummelling in rage, unable to control the stream of bad language I didn't think I knew.

Although surprised by the attack, the man quickly recovered. I was no match for him. With a powerful sweep of his arm he brushed me aside, sending me sprawling on to the fence. My bellow ended in a gasp as the bolt-cutters, held low in his hand, connected with my stomach. I heard my clothes rip on the barbed wire that topped the fence as I doubled up and slid to the ground.

There were other sounds, too, only vaguely accounted for through my pain — indistinguishable shouts, pounding footsteps, revving engines, all amplified by the still night air.

'Lyndal! Are you all right?'

I was cradled in Hugh's arms, held tight against his chest, comforted by the frantic kisses on my forehead.

'Are they getting away?' I asked, each word an effort of shallow breathing.

'Yes, my darling, but don't think about that now. This is more important. Where does it hurt? We've got to get you home where we can look at this properly.' He turned his head and called, 'Grant, bring the car!'

7

Although I protested I could walk unaided, that it wasn't my feet that hurt, Hugh and Grant insisted on supporting me until we reached the part of the glassed-in veranda farthest from my parents' room.

It wasn't only my bruised body and the need for quiet that prevented me talking about the night's events. My impulsive action had wrecked the chances of nailing the sheep stealers, probably scaring them out of the district altogether. I told myself that would be a good thing, but I knew catching them with a load of our sheep on board would have been a better result.

Another thing kept me quiet. It was hard to admit Hugh and Grant had been right, not only about the timing of the attempted raid.

'I know who it was,' I said at last, swallowing my pride.

There was no surprise on my brother's face, no hint of smugness, either. I couldn't see Hugh's response. He was behind me, meticulously dabbing stinging disinfectant on the numerous punctures made by the barbed wire across my upper arm and back. Except for asking were my tetanus shots up-to-date, he hadn't spoken since coming into our house.

'He uses a very distinctive after-shave,' I added.

My brother nodded, still not saying anything. I wondered if they were waiting for a more detailed apology from me. I twisted around to include Hugh, forcing him to cease his ministrations.

'I'm sorry I — '

'Acted so impulsively?' my brother said. 'That's you all over, Sis. You could've been seriously hurt, you know.'

Although we'd been speaking in low tones, it had been enough to disturb my father, a notoriously light sleeper. He appeared at the sun-room door, a quizzical look on his face.

'What's going on, Grant?'

'Nothing, Dad,' I answered for my brother. 'Just winded myself, not serious.'

'At this time of the night? It must be nearly morning.'

He came farther into the room, his glance taking in my dishevelled state. I hastily shrugged my shirt back on.

'We were fox-hunting and I fell out of the truck,' I lied.

It was a weak, spur-of-the-moment excuse, meant to deflect him until we decided how much to tell of Jason Dunstan's perfidy. Perhaps he need never know. No sheep had been stolen, and hopefully Jason would fade from our lives. I, for one, would be happy to forget he'd ever been in mine.

My father's attention was drawn to Hugh.

'And who's this? One of your friends, Grant?'

Grant found his voice.

'Oh, yes, Dad, this is my mate, Hugh. As Lyndal said, we've been . . . we've been spotlighting for foxes. Nothing much happened until Lyndal fell off the back of the truck.'

He laughed nervously and indicated my torn clothes. But my father only gave my injuries what I considered was a cursory glance. He was interested in Hugh. Suddenly, the air crackled with tension.

'I was sure I'd discovered a fox lair at the foot of Little Budginini Hill. Seems I was wrong.'

I was babbling, just as nervous as Grant, fearful of what would happen if our father discovered Hugh's identity. My stomach knotted and unknotted painfully.

'One of your mates you say, Grant?'

A suspicious note had crept into Dad's voice.

'Yes, Dad. This is Hugh.'

There was another long, tense pause. I hadn't seen any other member of

Hugh's extended family but obviously Dad had. His face changed.

'You're a Trevellyn,' he accused.

'How do you do, sir?' Hugh said, stepping forward with hand out-stretched.

Dad ignored it.

'What are you doing in my house?' he demanded, his face mottled with rage.

If Hugh had thought I exaggerated my father's feelings toward the Trevellyns, he could be in no doubt now. But it didn't change his inherent good manners.

'I am a friend to both Grant and Lyndal,' he began reasonably, without dropping his extended hand.

'I won't have you in my home,' my father raged, taking a threatening step towards Hugh, his fists clenched.

'Dad, don't!' I cried, but it was too late.

Dad's face changed yet again, this time into a violent spasm of pain. He clutched at his chest, and pitched forward into Hugh's arms.

At that moment, my mother appeared. She gave a choking cry and ran across the room as Hugh laid my father on the couch.

'His tablets!' she urged, pushing Hugh aside to dive her hand into the pocket of my father's dressing-gown.

Completely opening his mouth, she forced a tablet under his tongue, held his jaw closed and stared hopefully down at his face. But Hugh wasn't waiting for a response. He turned to me.

'Lyndal, get blankets and pillows,' he said before addressing my mother. 'Mrs Frazer, I think you should get dressed right away.'

He took out his mobile phone, tapped in a number, and after a short wait, spoke.

'Dad? We need to get Alex Frazer to hospital as soon as possible. Looks like a heart attack. Could you ready the plane?'

Hugh glanced out into the night.

'Should be first light soon, at least

enough for take-off. I'll alert the Mobile Intensive Care ambulance as soon as you're in the air. Be with you in about twenty minutes, half an hour at the outside.'

I hadn't moved.

'Take-off? You asked your father to fly Dad to hospital in his plane?' I asked, incredulously.

'Yes, why not? Now, the blankets and pillows, please, Lyndal.'

Why not? Because his father was a Trevellyn, that was why not! I couldn't believe a Trevellyn would do that for a Frazer.

My mother was dressed, an overnight bag at her feet, when I came back into the room.

'You stay here with Grandmama, Lyndal,' she said.

'But I want to go with you,' I protested.

'There isn't room in the plane,' Hugh explained, hardly pausing in his preparations. 'Grant needs to go to look after your mother. I'll come back here as soon as they're in the air.'

With unhurried efficiency, he and Grant wrapped Dad in the blankets and eased him into the station-wagon Grant had backed up to the veranda steps in readiness. I followed with the pillows. Hugh's calm exterior only faltered when he came to kiss me goodbye.

'I'm sorry, Lyndal, darling,' he murmured before reluctantly breaking away and getting behind the wheel.

There wasn't a chance to ask was he sorry I was being left behind, or sorry he'd brought on my father's attack. Through tear-filled eyes, I watched the tail-lights disappear down the driveway.

'He seems a very nice young man. I feel confident he'll take good care of your father,' Grandmama said at my side.

I hadn't heard her come out of the house. I turned to look at her. Despite the early hour, she was fully dressed, immaculate as ever. I couldn't imagine anything bringing her from the bedroom in a dressing-gown, except fire, perhaps.

The kitchen was warm and welcoming. Grandmama began preparing an early breakfast. My mother had left me to look after her, but it seemed Grandmama was going to look after me. I was glad. The night's events had caught up with me. I felt drained of all emotion and my whole body ached. I searched in the medicine cupboard for a painkiller.

'I presume that was your secret letter-writer. Where does he live?'

That stopped me. Had Grandmama read Hugh's letter after all? I probably wouldn't ever know the truth but it no longer seemed important enough to ask. The worst that could happen had happened.

'Didn't you recognise him?' I asked rather needlessly, my mind already diverted from my aches and pains.

'No, it was too dark. Should I have?'

'Well, Dad did.'

The toaster popped. She took her time, fussing about for a toast rack, quartering the bread, bringing out the marmalade before pushing both across the table toward me. I was impatient, and hungry, not for food but for more facts about the Trevellyns. Perhaps Grandmama would be prepared to tell me the cause of the feud.

'Whatever happened?' I demanded, ignoring the toast.

'What do you mean?' she asked, untroubled by my aggressive tone.

I was tired and 'way beyond being frightened of her likely displeasure.

'Grandmama, don't play games with me! Hugh and I love each other but you can see what happened when Dad laid eyes on him. What kind of a future do you think we have? I'll tell you. None! And why? Because of some stupid feud.'

I wasn't prepared for the bewilderment that registered on her face.

'Was that what your father's turn was about? Clarice came and woke me but

140

didn't tell me any more than the bare details.'

'Yes. You know how he goes on about the Trevellyns. When he saw Hugh — '

'Your young man is a Trevellyn?'

I'd never known my grandmother to interrupt someone when they were speaking. I stared at her. She went white, gave a strangled groan and covered her face with blue-veined hands.

The once-proud figure swayed alarmingly on her feet before slumping down into the nearest chair. Dismayed, I pushed mine back and hurried to kneel beside her.

'I didn't mean for Dad to see him. He had promised to stay away but I had an accident and . . . Grandmama, what is it?'

'Hugh Trevellyn? Oh, no, Lyndal! What have I done? If anything happens to your father it will be my fault.'

'Your fault? How do you mean? I don't understand. It was him seeing Hugh that brought it on. How can that be your fault? More likely mine, for having fallen in love with the wrong person.'

Grandmama shook her head from side to side, almost as if she hadn't heard me.

'It is all my fault,' she insisted. 'I caused the feud, and I am guilty of keeping it alive, for sixty-two years.'

Guilty? My grandmother? What could she have done that was so bad? She'd always lived by such a strict set of rules, and expected everyone else to do the same. It just didn't seem possible. I sat back on my heels, my mind refusing to take it in, unable to think of anything to say.

At last, she straightened her back and looked into my face.

'You say you and Hugh are in love?'

There was only one answer to that.

'Yes.'

'Then I have to end it.'

'I'm not giving up Hugh.'

The very thought, too horrible to contemplate, made me cut rudely across her remark before she'd finished.

'No, no, I mean end the feud. I must tell your father the truth!'

Her voice faltered as if overwhelmed by the very idea, then strengthened with determination.

'Just as soon as he is better. Yes, I must do that for you. I will tell him.'

End the feud? That seemed too good to be true. But even as my hopes began to rise, my confused mind was struggling with her talk of guilt. It didn't make sense. What was the truth she said she had to tell my father that would make a difference? I needed to know.

Restlessly, Grandmama made to get up out of her chair. I put a hand on her arm to restrain her.

'When he's better, Grandmama, but you must tell me, too. You can't not tell me. We're talking about my future.'

The grandmother who considered my plea was so different from the stern matriarch I'd know all my life, now softer, more human.

'You're right, Lyndal,' she said after

another long silence. 'But I don't know where to begin, it was all so long ago.'

'Just begin at the beginning,' I suggested, all my anger dissipated by her obvious distress.

I got up off my haunches and began to make coffee, to give her time to compose herself. I finished before she began speaking, hesitantly at first, then more strongly.

'My father and Mr Frazer had a connection through mutual friends. The family, that is, my parents, my sister and I, came from the city to stay at Balool for the Picnic Races. We were only girls, younger than you are now, and everything about the outback was exciting. There were two Frazer boys, Alexander and Colin, so we had a good time socially, visiting surrounding homesteads for parties.'

Grandmama thanked me for the cup of coffee I put in front of her but left it untouched.

'Tirra Lirra was one of those

properties, but by far the most impressive. It covered hundreds of acres of prime land, with a magnificent riverside mansion unlike any other in the district. And Hugh, the eldest son of the family, was everything a girl could desire in a husband. Not only was he rich and handsome but he was tipped to follow his father into Parliament. A most suitable match for any girl, and I decided I would be that girl.'

There was a long silence as Grandmama re-lived her memories. By the look on her face I could see they weren't particularly happy ones.

'Did you fall in love with him?' I prodded.

If the first Hugh Trevellyn was anywhere near as handsome as my Hugh she surely must have.

'What's that?' she asked absentmindedly.

'I asked if you fell in love. You did, didn't you?'

She hesitated.

'No, I didn't,' she insisted, 'but I told

myself that would come with time. I was determined to be Mrs Hugh Trevellyn. I did everything possible to outdo the competition from the local girls, using the Frazer boys shamefully.'

It was hard to imagine Grandmama as a predatory young woman. She had always frowned on any suggestion of making the running, even in fun. One must wait to be approached by a man, she claimed.

'The night of the ball at Tirra Lirra I went too far. We were leaving the next day to return to the city and I hadn't achieved my goal, which was an engagement ring. I was desperate, and clung to Hugh's arm, using every pretext I could. It was a shocking display of forward behaviour, and quite foolish.'

I wondered if it was as bad as Grandmama made out. She was so old-fashioned. I was going to say so when she went on.

'Especially when Hugh announced that night he was going to marry one of the local girls. Everyone was looking at me. That was when your grandfather stepped up, took my hand and announced our engagement also.'

I was flabbergasted.

'Without asking you?'

'Yes, it was such a gallant thing to do. It saved me from public humiliation.'

'But why did you marry Grandfather? Why didn't you just go back to the city and forget all about it?'

'In my day, we didn't put so much emphasis on marrying for love as you young people do, more's the pity,' Grandmama answered, her old self peeping through. 'A good marriage was very important. Although Alexander Frazer wasn't as suitable a match as a Trevellyn, my parents were pleased. And I was preparing to be a good wife and mother, even if I didn't love him then.'

She got up out of her chair and took the cold coffee to the sink. I followed her.

'The feud, what about the feud?

There must've been more to it than that,' I persisted, afraid the stream of reminiscence would dry up before I learned the whole truth.

She turned and stood facing me, almost defiantly.

'To save my pride, I told Alexander that Hugh had led me on, to the point of . . . being . . . familiar with me. I hadn't realised how idealistic Alexander was. In a white-hot rage he accused Hugh and . . . '

She fluttered her hands in a tiny gesture of futility.

'I couldn't take it back and lose my husband's respect, and in turn, my son's when he was old enough to have been told this by his father. It's been hard keeping the secret all these years.'

'Tell me about keeping secrets,' I muttered, thinking about my efforts to keep my love for Hugh from my father. No wonder Hugh knew nothing about the feud. It was one-sided, a Frazer feud, handed from father to son, a secret from the present-day

Trevellyns. That reminded me.

'But why had Dad become almost paranoid about the Trevellyns after all these years?' I asked.

It took a little while for Grandmama to return to the present and answer my question.

'I think it's common in heart patients that everything is exaggerated. They become fearful of dying.'

Panic rose in me.

'He's not going to die, is he, Grandmama?'

'No, darling,' Hugh answered from the outside doorway. 'He'll be ill for a while. They won't be able to put off the bypass any longer. It's a tough operation, but he'll get through. He's tough, too.'

I had been so engrossed in Grandmama's story I hadn't heard Hugh's car returning from Tirra Lirra. My immediate delight in seeing him standing there was quickly overshadowed by familiar apprehension.

I looked back at my grandmother.

She stood stock-still for a long time, staring across the room at Hugh. I didn't realise I was holding my breath until she gave a slight nod, almost to herself, and I exhaled with a sigh.

'You're very like your grandfather, Hugh,' she said at last, with a smile that told me she hadn't forgotten her first love.

8

Spring came quickly to Balool after that, and my days were blissfully happy.

True to her word, Grandmama put things right for Hugh and me. Until she did that I hadn't allowed my hopes to rise. Sixty-two years was a long time to live a lie. Would she find it too hard to face Dad when the time came?

Hugh drove us both to Wagga after my father was out of danger and well enough to hear her story. She came from his hospital room looking shaken, and every one of her eighty years. But the news was good. Dad's brush with death had given him a new perspective of life. He wanted nothing but my happiness.

I couldn't hold it against Grandmama that she'd allowed the feud to carry over into my generation. She wasn't to know how her shame would affect my life. In fact, I admired her for having the courage to tell my father the truth when she realised that. It couldn't have been easy.

Despite her denial, it was plain by the way she looked at Hugh that she had loved his grandfather. Being rejected must have really hurt. But, instead of going back to the city and putting it all behind her, she had married his neighbour, Alexander Frazer.

Was that so she could at least be near him? I could understand that. But if that was so, her face-saving lie to her husband put an end to the dream. It was a sad story and I had to wonder if Grandfather Frazer's ban was imposed more out of jealousy than high-minded outrage, and to wonder if old Hugh Trevellyn had ever regretted his choice of a wife.

I asked Hugh if his grandparents had been happy.

'How would I know?' he answered. 'I was only a kid when they went to live in the city and left my father in charge of

Tirra Lirra. But I'm not a kid anymore,' he teased, giving me a very grown-up kiss to prove it.

Hugh and my father had come to an understanding.

'He seems an all right sort of bloke, very resourceful,' was Dad's under-stated way of approving of my choice of partner, when it came my turn to visit.

'An all right sort of bloke?' I repeated. 'He saved your life, Dad.'

'Yes, yes, I know and I've thanked him for that.'

He gave me a sly grin.

'A steady chap like him might be good for you. Curb your impulsiveness, perhaps?'

We both laughed at that. Despite the tangle of medical attachments that made it awkward, my father reached out to embrace me and soften the criticism.

'I'll be glad to get out of here,' he complained gruffly as he settled back against the pillows.

It was his way of covering his show of

emotion, I guessed.

'And we'll be glad to have you home. We miss you.'

I was becoming emotional myself by this time so hurried on to talk of more mundane things.

'There's a lot going on at Balool, what with shearing starting Monday.'

My father's remark about my impulsiveness in no way referred to the night of his heart attack. Grant and I decided not to tell him of the sheep-stealing attempt, nor of Jason's part in it. Because I moved too quickly that night we had nothing more than suspicions that wouldn't stand up in court. In fact, if we voiced them we could well end up in court ourselves, charged with libel.

Although Jason visited my father in hospital, our paths hadn't crossed, and from what I heard in the township, they wouldn't in the future. The Policeman had transferred back to the city. I was glad to hear that, not sure how I could have controlled myself in a face-to-face situation. I was still angry at how I'd been used.

'All present and correct,' Grant announced the day the sheep shearing ended as he added up the shearers' tallies and wrote out the contractor's cheque.

We toasted the completion of the biggest job of the year, looking out over the green paddocks dotted with newly-shorn sheep. The caravan of shearers' vehicles was hardly out of sight before I began making wedding plans.

'This shearing-shed will need a good clean,' I pronounced, noting the stray wisps of wool caught on the rough timber of the building, and the spider webs that festooned out-of-the-way corners.

Grant groaned.

'Does it have to be done right away? I'm looking forward to at least one day off.'

He looked around.

'I don't see much wrong with it. After all, it is a shearing-shed.'

'Not good enough for a wedding reception.'

That made him sit up and take notice!

'Has Hugh asked you to marry him?'

'Well, no, not officially but I'm sure he will.'

My brother grinned.

'And I'm sure he will, too,' he said. 'If he doesn't he'll have me to answer to. What's stopping him?'

'Oh, he's waiting for the right moment,' I answered confidently.

When that moment came I was caught unawares. It was the first day Dad was home from hospital. Hugh's father, Jack, flew him to Tirra Lirra and the Trevellyns joined us at Balool for a traditional Sunday roast. It was the first time I'd met my future in-laws.

All morning I'd been in a tizz, unable to make up my mind over what to wear for the occasion. In the end, I decided they should see me as I was most days and chose a crisp white shirt and new jeans.

We lingered around the table until late in the afternoon, refilling the coffee pot several times as we got to know each other. At last, Hugh stood up and reached for my hand.

'Why don't we go for a ride?' he asked, waiting for my agreement before excusing us from the family.

The knowing smiles exchanged by Jack and Barbara Trevellyn should have alerted me . . .

9

The sun was sinking as we rounded Little Budginini Hill. We slipped out of our saddles, and, leaving the horses to graze, climbed the outcrop, choosing to sit on the largest of the smooth rocks at the summit. The beginning of a night wind blew cool in our faces but enough of the heat of the day remained stored in the stones to warm our bodies.

Below us, the silver river snaked across the wide plain between Balool and Tirra Lirra.

'Dad and Mum want to retire to the city,' Hugh began. 'I will be left in charge.'

'That'll be a big job,' I murmured, not surprised by the news.

Obviously handing over management was a tradition in the Trevellyn family.

'Yes.'

There was a long, companionable

silence as we stared into the darkening distance. I thought about the large homestead at Tirra Lirra that had captivated Grandmama all those years ago. It was time to fill its many rooms with a new generation of children, our children.

'Too big for one man on his own,' Hugh went on, as if he was thinking about the same thing.

'But you won't be on your own,' I protested impulsively. 'I'll be — '

As soon as the words were out I wished I hadn't said them. The stillness of the body beside mine warned me I may have gone too far. My confidence faltered.

Until now, it hadn't occurred to me that Hugh's feelings could've changed. I realised nothing had been said between us about our future since our unexpected meeting at the Netball Association's Conference. I'd refused to make a commitment then because of my father's illness. That was a long time ago. Could I be sure he still felt the same way about getting married?

'I'll be here,' I ended lamely, unable to look at him.

The moment of embarrassment was short-lived. Hugh reached for me with a shout of delight.

'There you go, impulsive as ever! You couldn't wait for me to ask you to marry me!'

He hugged me and buried his face in my hair.

'I love that about you. Don't ever change,' he begged in a husky voice.

Whether impulsiveness was a desirable lifelong character trait seemed unimportant to me right then. I was more interested in the first part of his declaration.

'Were you about to ask me to marry you?' I prompted.

'Of course I was. You said you couldn't consider it while your father was ill. The operation has been successful, he has recovered. As well, the imaginary feud is over, so there is nothing to stand in our way. But I did want to ask you formally, you know.'

'Well, you still can,' I retorted cheekily, all doubts gone.

He let go of me and moved quickly to kneel at my feet and take both my hands in his. The wind played with a stray lock of hair that fell across his forehead.

He had never looked more handsome, or more serious. I became serious, too. The grip on my hands tightened.

'Lyndal, I love you. Since the first time I saw you I've known I wanted to spend the rest of my life with you. Will you marry me?'

There was a slight tremor in his deep voice that thrilled me. Happiness was welling up inside me, a smile tugging at the corners of my mouth. I thought of the day we'd met when Hugh rescued me from the river. A future with him had been the last thing on my mind then. I was cold and wet and on Tirra Lirra land. Now he was no longer a forbidden love and his dream of us being together was about to come true. I leaned forward and put my lips on his.

'Yes,' was all I could say before Hugh responded enthusiastically.

Some time later, I remembered his shaky voice and put a question to him.

'You seemed almost nervous about asking me to marry you. Surely you didn't think I'd say no?'

'Well, you haven't actually said you love me . . . ' he began.

I stopped that nonsense with another kiss.

'I love you, love you, love you,' I assured him, repeating myself, unnecessarily as it happened.

His wide smile told me once would have been enough.

THE END